Tarnished Angels

By Michael Paterson-Jones

About the author

Michael Paterson-Jones was born in the UK but went to Africa as a baby. He grew up in Kenya and Rhodesia - now Zimbabwe. He went to university in South Africa. His career started as an agronomist, to industrial chemist, teacher and professor.

He married his Rhodesian born artist and illustrator wife, Thora, in 1970. That year they bought a coffee farm in The Vumba mountains on the Mozambique border and lived there for seven years through the "Bush War". They travelled extensively in Mozambique.

They then moved to South Africa firstly to Cape Town and then to Durban. After twenty two years in South Africa and in Swaziland as an academic, he and Thora lived for seven years in Upstate New York before returning to the UK where they currently reside.

Michael's passion for writing is not a new one. He has penned many words to paper from journals, to scientific papers, to children's books and newspaper columns.

Set in the 1980's, Tarnished Angels is a fast moving tale of two feisty, strong-willed young women, Boncherie Armatrading and Consuela Bojangles and their quest for justice for an orphanage close to their hearts and the place that ignited their initial bond. We meet Michael John – a hardened, weathered ex Selous Scout.

The story starts in London and rapidly moves to South Africa. Action-packed adventure including an endurance motor race builds suspense throughout the pages. Next stop is Zimbabwe not long after independence. From Zimbabwe the story moves onto the coast of Mozambique and involvement in the local war. Finally, a yacht trip with the protagonists takes them to the Natal coast of South Africa. Fascinating and exciting characters drive the story forward, immersing you in the fast-paced, spell-binding twists and turns in the tale. The conclusion to this tale takes our characters back to Britain, with an unexpected twist at the end...

Chapter 1

The Thunderhead, born above the Mozambique Channel, sailed slowly towards the single kopje that stood sentinel-like on the Msasa tree dotted plain. Some rays of the setting sun disguised the dark base of the cumulus cloud in shades of pink and purple. Others danced on the green, yellow, red and gold of the Msasa trees new seasons' growth. Others again, bounced off the granite crystals of the hand-hewn stone walls of the house. Massive as it was, the house on top of the kopje was dwarfed as it stood between huge boulders of the parent rock.

A mountain of a man sat on the patio, seemingly indifferent to the approaching storm. Any movement of his great body was accompanied by rippling of the thick layer of subcutaneous fat that imprisoned him. His flaccid hand tipped with effeminately long nails caressed the arm of the beautifully built young black who posed beside his chair. Behind him an exact copy of the first Shona youth fanned him gently in an effort to alleviate the high heat and humidity that inevitably attended the summer season's rains.

His small, dark, piggish eyes peered out of craters of fat at the telegram that lay opened on the mosaic topped table. With his free hand, he raised the crystal glass of kummel. He sipped and savored the sweet caraway seed liqueur then spoke. From hairless lips came excited high-pitched words, "Nearly there, my black beauties. Another two million in Zürich! Soon, we can all leave this godforsaken country and surround ourselves with culture and beautiful things in a clean and civilized Europe. Ah! the thought of it!"
Narcissus and Adonis did not reply, nor was it expected of them.

*****

Rain slid down the consecrated slates, skimmed the overflowing gutter and, after free-falling for a few metres, scored a direct hit between the ecclesiastical collar and a sun shy neck. The factors determining the event were linked. The rain, a natural enough phenomenon had timed his arrival to add to the feeling of impending doom experienced by the old priest. The blocked gutter on the chapel roof was indicative of the parlous state of the church's finances and the target presented to the falling rain owed its existence to the worry-browed, grey-haired head of Father O'Meara.

He left the comparative shelter of the chapel roof overhang and, head still inclined, crossed the courtyard. Inside his study the necessity to restore his thermal equilibrium made him open the top drawer of his desk and extract an almost full bottle of Irish whiskey.

'The warming process might as well start from within' thought the old priest.

Having settled a fair dollop of spirit upon the mucous lining of his stomach, he removed his coat and endeavoured to dry the back of his shirt with the anti-macassar from the back of the chair. He pulled the same chair in front of the empty fireplace and sat so as to feel its symbolic warmth.

He centred his thoughts on the financial bombshell dropped by Manny less than an hour ago. Manny was apologetic, extremely so, but he had made it quite clear that his own, suddenly precarious financial position had forced him to serve notice that the unsecured, interest-free mortgage he held on St Mark's orphanage would have to be redeemed within three months.

Financial crises were nothing new to Father O'Meara, since the continued existence of St Mark's had been on an ongoing scrimp and

save experience for the 40 years of his service to a succession of homeless children. But the matter of finding £150,000 at such short notice appeared to be an impossible task.
Prayer he had tried but perhaps his preoccupation with the material had precluded successful communication with the good Lord. Earlier, sitting in the front pew of the chapel he had excused a communication breakdown with the thought that 'the Lord helps them who help themselves'.

As the spirit, alcoholic that is, coursed through his hardened veins, a smile crept across his face and he said aloud to the clock above the fireplace, "the Lord will also help them who are smart enough to arrange for somebody else to help themselves. Doesn't make sense but I know what I mean! The girls, me darling blessed little sinning saints, that's the answer!"

*****

Across the moisture-shrouded city, sheets of rain shattered against the window pane, regrouped and running snail-trail like down the glass and window sill, dropped to the ground to waste wetly away on the pavement. On the dryer, warmer, lighter side of the window, two young women were busy idling away an evening at home. The taller of the two sat cross-legged and naked on the duvet of a double bed. She was occupied in applying little red hearts to fingernails recently painted black. The effect, though perhaps not a claimant to any degree of subtlety, was striking and thus befitted the owner of the startling nails. A woman in her mid-twenties with long blonde air, cornflower blue eyes and a figure guaranteed to put a gender-bender on the straight and narrow.

Her flat mate and visitor from the adjoining bedroom was dressed in a black, decorated kimono. She sat on an easy chair with legs up on the double bed. Her urchin styled hair framed a face more sallow in complexion than the others, with brown almond shaped almost oriental eyes. This face, more Tretchikovian in beauty than that of her companion, topped a body less voluptuous but nonetheless alluring; compact, shorter limbs, smaller breasts and narrow waist. She occupied herself with a Scientific American journal.

Neither spoke and the only sound was the alien emotive strains of an Ivanov Ipolitov piece that issued from the music centre in the corner. The dulcet tones of the piano surrendered to the strident rings of the bedside telephone. After the third ring the blonde lay back across the bed and reaching over her head, removed the handset from its cradle. The loud Irish voice that billowed from the earpiece left neither of the room's occupants in doubt as to its owner. When the verbal barrage had died down, the blonde replied in honeyed words, "Father dear, you are a humbug. My soul is in no greater danger tonight than at any other time, but, since for some inexplicable reason I love you, I'll come to confession, your confession, as soon as I can get there". With an exasperated smile she put the phone down.
She addressed the other, "O'Meara's is in trouble again and wants to see us both now. Let's get dressed and move."
"So be it" came the reply.
Fifteen minutes later the two stepped into a red Lotus Esprit Turbo and proceeded from Queens Gardens via Queensgate and the Bayswater Road in the direction of London's east end.

*****

More should be said about the two on their way to St Mark's in Cheapside. The label on the post box in the foyer of the expensive block of flats in Queens Gardens proclaimed them to be Boncherie Armatrading and Consuela Bojangles. These names, applied to the blond and the brunette respectively, were as false as they were outrageous.

To seek their origin, one must turn the clock back 10 years, give or take a few months, and meet two nearly 16-year-old inmates of St Mark's orphanage. To the two unwanted waifs the orphanage represented home, a life of hardship, discipline, regimentation and pain inflicted by the indomitable Mother Kathleen but tempered by the love and affective humanity of a then younger and more visionary Father O' Meara. Cheryl Armour and Constance Brown lived and laughed and cried their earlier years away within the high wall confines of the orphanage. The gradual event of womanhood marked on them a need to spread their wings and fly the restrictions of the religious home. They flexed their flight feathers in illicit visits to the outer world of cosmopolitan London. An unlocked garden gate was the door to freedom from which they would sally forth after dark in violent plumage of garish miniskirts and copious amounts of misapplied make up. Mother Kathleen snored on in blissful ignorance and father O'Meara turned a deaf ear to the nocturnal creak of the garden gate and sipped more of the health giving water of Erin.

The test flights increased in frequency and duration until one fateful day, the fledglings fled the brick and mortar nest in Cheapside altogether. Consider the events that preluded this momentous move. The weather was inclement and a re-run of James Dean's "East of Eden" provided the girls with the means of passing an entertaining and cosy evening.

In the dark they sat chewing gum, the "devil's saliva" according to Mother Kathleen, and let their minds wander outside the banality of their lives. The evening could have passed without achieving historic import if a middle-aged, middle-of-the-road, stolid Lancastrian

gentleman had not reached a climax of excitement on his first visit to London and placed a somewhat pudgy hand on the fairly substantial expanse of bare flesh which extended beyond Cheryl's mini and represented her thigh. In storybooks, damsels in distress seem to have a predisposition to do one of two things, they either swoon, that is, medically speaking suffer syncope, or alternatively pollute the air with mega-decibelic discordant cries of help. Cheryl did neither. Perhaps few graduates from an orphan's rude school of life qualified as "damsels". She removed his hand and placing her lipstick begrimed lips close to a rather hirsute ear hissed sharply,
"Try that again mate, and I'll break your bloody fingers."
A series of north country mutters of apparently sincere apology came muffled from a quickly reddening face, visible even in the twilight of the cinema.

Towards the end of the interval, as the lights flickered then dimmed again, Fred Kershaw sidled past the multiple hazards of a dozen extended knees and regained his seat. Without a word he passed to his left numerous peace offerings. A Coke, two boxes of chocolates, a bag of popcorn and an ice cream. A split-second hesitation only and Cheryl accepted the sugarcoated olive branch.
"Ta mate," she murmured and, in accordance with the tradition of many years standing, passed half of the gastronomic treasure trove to her sister- in- want on the left, Constance. The Lancashire lard barrel followed them from the foyer into the winter shrouded Street. From behind, he addressed Cheryl,
"I know I didn't ought to have done it but you're a right perky lass."
"Beat it pop" came the reply.
Thirty years of scratching and scrambling his way to a position at the top of the cotton industry were evidence of a dogged persistence in the man from the north and he was not easily put off
"Cum on luv, how about a nice cuppa char and some cake at that café over there?"
Again, a split-second hesitation, "We're together" she said, her thumb

indicating Connie standing beside her.
"That's all right. More the merrier, they say" he beamed.
Sitting in the brightly lit café, the girls forsook conversation with their benefactor, as ones until now strangers to affluence, compensated fully. As a starving man becomes addicted to dry bread so the two girls, starved of anything that smacked of indulgence or luxury, sold not their souls but their bodies to the god of abundance. It was a slow, progressive sale. Fred Kershaw's excursions to the big city were initially only at monthly intervals. By arrangement he met them on a Friday night after he had concluded the business that brought him to London and took them to the cinema or the theatre and they never crept back into the orphanage hungry. The girls talked of their futures and saw the bleakness of another two years in the orphanage. Their devotion to each other compensated but they saw, in the open walleted devotion of that funny accented devotee, a way to real freedom.

As soon as the girls turned sixteen, both within the space of a week, they made their move. On the planned Friday they crept through the garden gate for the last time, each carrying in a duffle bag their meager possessions. They met Fred outside the Odeon Leicester Square and instead of entering the said edifice steered him into a quiet restaurant nearby. Connie broke the silence that followed the departure of the waiter take in their order.
"Mr. Kershaw, to start with we are both sixteen now and we're going to start calling you Fred. Next, we know you're pretty loaded and we want your help. There's no way we're going back to the orphanage. Before you say no, let me tell you the plan we have for all of us." Fred took a swig of beer and waited.
It was Bonnie who continued; "If you're as well-heeled as you say, you can rent us a flat and give us an allowance. We're both over sixteen now and aren't "jailbait" any more so we are prepared to let you have a bit more than the feeling, groping and pinching we've let you do so far. There's only one condition we come as a pair and you treat us exactly the same, no favourite, okay?"

Fred choked on his beer and the froth that rose in front of his face held two almost simultaneous visions. In one he saw his wife, at the moment safely ensconced in Dukinfield, towering over him as ever, needling and pushing with the affectionless single-mindedness that had characterized twenty years of loveless marriage. Any suspicion of a ménage-a-trois far-flung from the connubial hearth would bring dreadful vengeance. This grey version was replaced with one of light and fun and happiness. Two naked nymphs skipped over a field of blue which on inspection revealed itself to be a giant bedspread. Visions gone, he drank deeply of the ale and came to a decision.

*****

Looking back over the years the arrangement had worked admirably. Fred's business unexpectedly expanded in the South and this meant more time away from Manchester. His wife remained on the scene to make certain portions of his life a misery but this was more than compensated for by the home from home that the girls created of the flat in Queens garden. Here he found life, love and even lust and passion freely given in quantities that strained his middle-aged heart. His illicit London nest cost a plenty as did the girls themselves but he never regretted the spending of a single penny of it. He shelled out enough for Bonnie and Connie, as he called them now, to study by correspondence and to explore the city steeped in history and art around them. The girls took new names which in their immaturity, they thought more fitting to their new more adult and glamorous selves. They were reborn as Boncherie and Consuela.
In the year that Bonnie and Connie passed their GCE "A" levels with flying colours, a steel hand crushed Fred's heart. It first made its presence known at the party the three threw to celebrate their

acceptance at university, Bonnie to read for a BA and Connie a BSc. The hand squeezed on in his is heart to the extent of putting Fred in extensive care at Guys for a week. Fred knew that his second double honeymoon was over. He still stayed at the flat in Queens garden as often as before but now he was happy to exchange bedroom frolics for slippers and dinner in front of the television and, in turn the girls were content to cater to his every need.

Bonnie and Connie cried at his funeral and cried again at the reading of his will. They cried not in fear of the awesome Mrs. Kershaw present, but in memory of their funny accented man who had loved them and lifted them, not out of the gutter, but out of the dismal daily drudge of the seemingly caring institution, the orphanage.

They were genuinely surprised to hear that the flat and all its contents was theirs, so long as they remained together and unmarried. In addition, provision had been made for an allowance of two thousand pounds a month. They had arrived. Both were now university graduates, one in the arts and one in chemistry and from their twin cocoons had emerged, if not 'lady' butterflies, at least not untutored, drab moths.

Expanding horizons including a new found love of fast cars and gambling. The latter was to provide them with a means to the manner to which they were determined to become accustomed.

Chapter 2

The three bowed heads of the individuals kneeling isolated in the pews did not move but Connie and Bonnie could feel the un-praying eyes that followed their passage to the confessional. The sight of both entering at the same time caused six eyebrows to rise and almost fall over the back of their heads. They sat in cramped discomfort. On the other side of the screen, Father O'Meara was conscious of their presence and, in contradiction to the ecclesiastical norms of privacy, thrust aside the curtain and pressed his unlovely, time-etched face to the wrought iron grill.

"Me darlings, you've come" came the words carried on a cloud of alcoholic fumes.

"For years now, in your blessing generosity you have helped me and St Mark's. For this, my children, I thank you and I offer a load of Hail Mary's and a ton of Our Fathers, but now, you sweet souls, I need your help more than ever before."

After a scarcely dignified hiccup he continued, "That blasted heathen Cohen wants his cursed one hundred and fifty thousand back and within three months so he ...."

Connie interrupted, "Father you're not being fair. It's his money and he's never charged you a cent of interest."

"I suppose you're right," mumbled the priest, "but what are we going to do now?"

Bonnie spoke, "We haven't got that kind of money at the moment but will fix something. Father go and put yourself to bed. We'll go and see Manny tomorrow and sort something out."

As they skirted the pews down the aisle of the chapel, the same three pairs of eyes followed them.

*****

Manny looked up as they entered his plush office at the back of the Kit Kat club. He stood up smiling and extended a hand dripping gold.
"Long time no see. It is vonderful you should be here to see an old man. But vot do you vant?"
It was Connie who replied,
"You bloody old skinflint, you know damn well what we want! We want to know why you suddenly want to put the screws on Father O'Meara!"
"Such half harsh words from vun so young and tender." smiled Manny
"It's not my choice but I have to do it. If I don't get the money I go down the drain.".
"That's impossible" exploded Connie "you're loaded!"
"I vish it was true," said the old Jew. "But I have taken a knock, just this last week. Would you that I go to jail so that that old booze ridden follower of the wrong Messiah can carry on living in such luxury?"
"That's not true," cried Bonnie
"All right, all right, but the fact remains that I have troubles, big troubles and vot must I do?" Many was almost pleading.
"Manny tell us what's the problem., Maybe we can help." Came from a puzzled Connie
"Okay okay! I tell you for what it's vorth."

Cohen's story came out. A couple of months ago a "gentleman", a South African by his accent, had started coming to the Kit Kat club regularly and playing the tables freely. He lost a lot but made up most of it on those nights that Lady Luck was his consort. Once he had become a familiar face in the gaming club he had approached Manny with a proposition. He had a parcel of emeralds, forty carats in all and all over one carat. They were Zimbabwean Sandawana emeralds and for sale well below their true value, at two hundred and fifty pounds a carat. He explained that they were rightfully his but he couldn't sell them openly as he had breached Zimbabwean exchange control regulations by removing them from that country. It was the only way he could get his money out.

Manny bought his story and the emeralds. They proved genuine and through his connections, Manny made a tidy profit. Over a period of a month, two more parcels of thirty to forty carats changed hands. Manny was well pleased. Then came the sucker punch. Tertius van der Westhuizen, as Manny knew him, offered him the balance of his emeralds for two million pounds. Manny hesitated, borrowed, mortgaged himself to the hilt and took the plunge.

Manny's buyer laughed at the last offering. To Cohen's intense discomfort, he explained that every one of the emeralds was flawless. In emeralds of one carat or more this is rare and in such a large quantity of stones, impossible. In other words, they were synthetic. Oh, the first three parcels were genuine enough but not the last big one. Cohen had been taken for a ride.

Van der Westhuizen had disappeared and Manny had to get down to the business of fighting for his financial life. The St Mark's one hundred and fifty thousand pounds was only part of the sum of money he had to find in three months' time as interest due on his borrowings. When Cohen had finished, his head hung down in sorrow and embarrassment.

"Wow!" gasped Bonnie, "When you make a boo-boo you do it in a big way, don't you, Manny?"

"Have you tried to get your money back, told the police or anything?" asked Connie.

Wringing his hands Cohen replied,

"That crook van der Westhuizen has disappeared and what should I tell the cops; I, the respectable Manny Cohen, pillar of the Temple David, a dealer in the bent goods? No, I must find a way to pay back my debts and I must have the money back from O'Meara."

The two women were silent for a minute. Then it was Connie who spoke, "Manny, if we get your money back, how about a ten percent commission?"

"If you can get my money back, I kiss your feet, mine dears," said a slightly brighter voice, "Mine vord is mine bond."

"Done" echoed two enthusiastic voices in unison.

Outside the club Bonnie asked of her companion with markedly less enthusiasm, "Blooming hell, what do we do now?"

"I think," said Connie, opening the driver's door of the red Lotus standing brazenly in a loading zone, "that we must do two things: firstly, raise some operating capital as we are a bit low on funds. Secondly we must find this van der Westgate whatever his name is."
"Oh, goody gumdrops! Another operation downfall, no?"
There's a new club just opened in Mayfair," enthused the brunette as she shoe-horned herself into the passenger seat of the car.

*****

The retired colonels monocle fell with a damp thud into his whiskey and soda and the waxed ends of a snow white moustache seemed to curl at least half a turn inwards. His buxom companion with a massive chest of such proportions that it resembled a China tea clipper in full sail, dug him in the ribs with the ivory handle of a furled fan (an accoutrement patently unnecessary in a cold bleak London).
"Edgar!" she boomed, "put your eyes back in their sockets."
"Yes M'dear," mumbled Edgar, "but by gad, what a sight!"
The sight was Bonnie and Connie as they slunk their way to the bar of the recently opened Vint-et-un Club. Tiers of plastic diadems dangled from a series of chandeliers which lit the falsely opulent bar. In their dazzling light the two women were a sight to behold. Connie was dressed in a high-necked, black lamé dress which seemed not to have been donned but to have been pre-shrunk around herself. Male heads turned, mouths gaped, heads swung a few degrees more, mouths gaped again at the sight of Bonnie, blonde hair piled high on her head and wearing what can best be described as a dressless evening strap. The red, short skirted satin creation stopped only microns above the sensors

line on her obviously bra-less ample bust.
"Your pleasures, mesdames?" queried the barman in a French accent as genuine as a three pound note.
"Vodkatini," from Connie
"Champagne cocktail!" from Bonnie.
As the Barman busied himself at his bacchanalian workbench, his two patrons surveyed, through an open arch, the scene in the next room where the action was. There were three roulette tables as well as blackjack and chemin-de-fer. The croupier at one of the roulette tables looked young and inexperienced, whereas the other two were obviously not. Mentally the two women noted this fact and whisperingly passed their observations to each other.
A vodkatini and champagne cocktail later, the two advanced on the cashier's cage and to his considerable surprise, Connie withdrew a pile of banknotes from her bag and plonked them down on the counter.
"Twelve thousand in hundred pound chips" requested the blonde.
On the way from the cashier's cage to the roulette table, Bonnie expressed doubt, "that's just about all that's left. I hope it works or we are going to be forced to work and I don't fancy that!"
"You sweet doubter, you do your bit and I'll do mine." said Connie confidently.
At the young croupier's table, Bonnie took up a standing position directly opposite him. Connie found a vacant seat approximately halfway round the table between them. She placed her handbag and chips in front of her and started to play. Bonnie meanwhile, just watched carefully. Connie's approach to the game, though seemingly casual, was all according to a prearranged plan. She placed bets ranging from four hundred to six hundred pounds at a time on the line between thirteen and fourteen.
Occasionally she increased her bets to one thousand pounds. After fifteen spins of the wheel, neither of the numbers had come up. On the sixteenth spin fourteen came up and, Connie pulled chips to the value of seven thousand eight hundred towards herself. Now came the big risk. Always using her left hand, she started placing bets of eight hundred to

fifteen hundred pounds on the same position on the table, but occasionally completely on either thirteen or fourteen. At the same time, she discreetly picked up five chips and concealed them in her right hand which rested on her lap.
Ten spins later, the pile of chips was almost gone. On the next spin she placed twelve hundred pounds on the boundary of thirteen and fourteen again.
The croupier called "Rien ne vas plus" and the wheel spun.
What happened next was Operation Downfall. In the last fraction of a second as the white ball was deciding whether to fall into thirteen or fourteen, Bonnie, with the timing of a seasoned thespian, threw her shoulders backwards. The effect of this was that two magnificent breasts popped into view above her non-too substantial dress. The ensuing result was electrifying. Men gasped in admiration, women in envy. The croupier was true to his gender. While his eyes were otherwise occupied, Connie quickly but unobtrusively pushed her pile of chips over the border into number thirteen and at the same time supplemented the pile of chips with five more. Bonnie apologizing profusely, put her treasures away. The croupier appeared slightly hesitant but counted Connie's chips and pushed a very much more substantial pile in her direction. To avoid suspicion, Bonnie left the room immediately and Connie reluctantly played for another twenty minutes and dropped some nine thousand pounds. The cashier offered Connie a cheque in preference to cash and the amount on the cheque made her smile. It was fifty one thousand five hundred pounds.

Here something should be said about Operation Downfall. The girls had come up with the idea two years previously. They had used it to make a substantial contribution towards their living expenses, but never used it more than once every six or so months, never more than once in the same gambling club and preferably only in one of the spate of new clubs there which seemed to mushroom in the capital at that time.
It was not foolproof. Manny Cohen was witness to this. He was one of their erstwhile victims or at least his club was. He happened to be

present at the tables on the night of the girls first visit to the Kit Kat Club and though not unappreciative of Bonnie's physical attributes, saw Connie's sleight of hand out of the corner of his eye. He made no public fuss, just quietly escorted the girls to his office. The matter was settled very amicably, the girls promising not to try Operation Downfall in his club again and the three of them flew to Antibes. A week later they returned; Manny to see an orthopaedic surgeon about his back but with an indelible smile on his face. The three had been firm friends ever since.

By prior arrangement the two troops regrouped after the successful operation. They met at the car in the underground parking garage around the corner from the Vingt-et-un. The Lotus purred its way up the ramp to where it met the street at ground level. It stopped for Connie to check the traffic in the street before turning right into the almost empty thoroughfare. The pair turned towards each other and giving the thumbs up signal to each other, grinned at the thought of a successful night work.
An over-coated, cloth capped figure stood on the pavement nearby waving a bundle of papers and shouted, his breath making smokeless rings in the cold early morning air.
"Piper, Piper. Read all about it!"

He stepped aside from the headline display board.
Both women stared at the headlines and felt as if they had been punched in the solar plexus.

Chapter 3

"MANNY *'HIGH STRAIGHT'* COHEN BRUTALLY SLAIN" screamed the headline. The Lotus remained stationary at the parking garage entrance and neither occupant spoke for several minutes.
"Impossible... he was alive this morning" croaked Bonnie.
"Why, why, I want to know? He couldn't have hurt a fly. He wouldn't make the Whitehouse Christmas card list, but he never hurt a single soul," griped Connie "I suppose that's bye-bye to St Mark's."
"I guess so." came the mournful reply.
Suddenly Connie got out of the car and ran down the street, "back in a sec!" she called over her shoulder. She ran as fast as her stiletto heels could carry her to a phone booth a block away. She fumbled in her bag for coins and dialed the Fleet Street number.
Bonnie could see that Connie's brown eyes were brimming with tears of rage as she got back into the car. Her knuckles showed white as she gripped the steering wheel and what she said came as angry gasps.
"Charlie Callan of The World filled me in... the bastard, the bloody bastard... it must be... he said the knife was a biltong knife... right in the bloody pump..."
"You mean" said Bonnie questioningly, "that he was stabbed with a knife only a South African would be likely to have, in other words, van der Westhuizen?"
"Yes" replied the tight-lipped Connie. She went on to say:
"Bonnie ten percent or no bloody ten percent commission, I reckon it's our duty to try and nail that son of a bitch... agreed?"
"You 're dammed right" came from Bonnie, now on the verge of tears.

*****

Manny must have had some friends upstairs, for on the day of his funeral, a wintry sun came out and an impromptu choir of robins sang as his remains were consigned to the earth.

Red-eyed and damp-cheeked the vengeful female pair had barely returned to the flat and put on the kettle, when the front door bell rang. "I'll get it", said Bonnie and opened the door to an unprepossessing young man, thin, about five foot three inches tall and wearing a large pair of horn-rimmed spectacles. In a series of stammers, he introduced himself. "I... I ...m... Max.... Co Co Co Cohen, Manny's son. I want to see you."

In accordance with his request Bonnie asked him in. Maxs' speech impediment seemed to have transferred itself to his feet as they also stammered in a away, or so it seemed, as he failed to negotiate the doormat and fell flat on his face behind Bonnie.

Tea seemed contra-indicated and rightly so as the newly broached bottle of whiskey worked wonders on the human wreck that represented Manny Cohen's only son and heir.

Three whisky tots later, he made his plea for help.

"Pop told me about you two. He said that you are going to help him get that money back and pay you a commission. Please carry on doing what he wanted. Otherwise, his estate will be declared insolvent and my Ma will have nothing. She's poorly. I'm not much use. I am still studying medicine, I suppose I could get a job, but please help clear my father's name. The people he borrowed the money from were good friends of the family."

Max's eyes and facial expression as he spoke pleaded his case more eloquently than what he said.

"My boy, we're going to give you a cheque for five thousand pounds for you and your Ma and we will give you our promise that we'll do our best. No guarantees, but we will do our best."

Max gave a pitifully grateful smile to the speaker, Connie.

Cheque in hand, whiskey in stomach, he amazingly renegotiated the doormat without tripping and took his leave. A loud silence followed,

broken only by the subdued tick of the ormolu clock on the mantelpiece. Eventually Connie re-opened communication:
"Peter the Pigeon!".
This apparently meaningless statement was as clear as crystal to Bonnie, for she replied with a slight expression of confidence edging her voice.
"Right, we'll start with him but I think we can also try the staff at the Kit Kat. They may have picked up something on van der Westhuizen."

*****

"Peter the Pigeon" Filmer's office was the end of the bar in the George and Dragon. Since it was past opening time, the office was open. He greeted the two women who took up the two stools next to him, with a smile that creased his face but did not encompass his eyes which remained hooded and hard.
"Customers or social" came from the thin lips.
In answer, Bonnie pushed an envelope along the bar towards him.
"Five hundred" she stated.
"My dear girl, the fee will depend on the service."
Filmer nevertheless took possession of the envelope, "ask and it shall be given."
"Manny...." Bonnie started.
"Ah yes the late departed. What about him?"
"We want his killer and bloody badly" came the reply.
"Expensive expensive" thin lips mouthed, and carried on to say, "the five hundred is up front. I'll bill you with the balance on delivery, same time tomorrow."
He terminated the interview by turning away, draining his drink and summoning the barman.

*****

As the Lotus sped towards the West End, seemingly unending drizzle caused ghostly halos to form round the street lights and the few pedestrians abroad in the early evening hunched their Macintosh collars tightly into their necks and scurried to their various destinations.

Surprisingly, the scene inside the Kit Kat appeared no different to any other night but, the general volume of sound seemed to be lowered in deference to the late owner of this palace of pleasure.
Connie and Bonnie made no move to take their customary place at the roulette tables but circulated separately and successively engaged the club staff in conversation. They probed and listened and mentally sifted through what was said. A possible break came when Connie stopped to talk with Vito, a small dark slick barman of Italian origin, who presided over the small bar in the roulette room.
"The big guy talksa funny huh, si, he comesa many times to my bar. He talksa about a nutting buta cars, racing cars. He say he race da Porche at Silverstone."
What Vito said initiated a train of thought in Connie's mind which prompted her next question.
"Vito, if he came here to race cars, he must have had some garage prepare his car. Did he perhaps say anything?"
Vito stared up in the air and considered the question. His eyes moved slowly from side to side, perhaps an outer and visible sign of mental activity. Finally, he spoke.
"It come to my head now. One night he said the son-of-a-beech mechanica no bloody good. He tink he change mechanica. He says he no go to the Competition Motors no more."
Connie's heart gave a leap. A start, the first piece in the jigsaw puzzle had fallen into place.
"You beautiful Spic, you've been a great help!" she cried as she passed a

fiver to the greasy haired immigrant.

Peter the Pigeon was apologetic, "I've got something but not much. I don't even know if it is worth five C's. You decide. Rumour has it, that it was a South African, van der Westhuizen."
Bonnie and Connie both knew that rumour in under-world parlance was not what it meant but was a statement of fact. They therefore accepted the statement for what it implied.
He continued:
"What I've told you isn't worth much. The yard could have told you the same but I've got a bit more. He skipped back to South Africa and he air-freighted his car, a Porsche with him. Also, I learnt that he put Manny down because Manny threatened to rock the boat over some dud stones, emeralds I believe."
Bonnie offered: "Peter, what you have told us is not really news but it's nice to know that we are on the right track. Keep the change."
With an aura of some optimism they left the smoke-filled room and returned to the flat. Over cups of instant coffee, they discussed their plans, made several phone calls and finally arrived at a decision. How long this took could be measured by the growing pile of gold tipped Sobranie cigarette ends in the ashtray that stood on the table between them. When Bonnie finally put the phone down, she and her companion looked well pleased.

Information so far gleaned, revealed that Tertius van der Westhuizen was a South African citizen who, over a period of years had been a regular visitor to Britain. Each time he came, he brought with him his Porsche and entered endurance races, and with some success. His car was always prepared for him by Competition Motors, a small specialist firm in Reading.

The proprietor of competition motors, Sid Haswell was inadvertently a mine of information. He volunteered the fact that though his firm was entrusted with the preparation of the car for each race van der

Westhuizen entered, they were surprisingly enough never allowed to collect the car from the airport. Van der Westhuizen always did this himself, which was unusual, as once he had delivered the car in Reading, he seemed to want nothing further to do with it except to take delivery at the appropriate race track, race it and return it to the care of the garage, until of course, when he claimed the Porsche for its transfer to some race venue in another European country.

From what Haswell said, it looked very much like van der Westhuizen was transporting emeralds, real or synthetic, hidden somewhere in the car, hence his insistence on taking delivery himself. Furthermore, it would appear that the money from the sale of the emeralds was removed from Britain to perhaps Switzerland, in the same car.
Haswell also revealed that van der Westhuizen was not short of money. What he earned in prize money from his sometime wins did not nearly cover the cost of transportation from South Africa and racing the car in Britain. It was transparently clear that van der Westhuizen, the racing driver and the powerful Porsche were nothing more than a clever means of transporting the emeralds one way and the proceeds of their sale another way.

However, van der Westhuizen did seem genuinely keen on motor racing, especially endurance races and a well-placed call to the secretary of the British Motor Racing Association, a friend of Bonnie's, brought to light the fact that the internationally recognized Castrol Nine Hour Endurance Race was due to take place in Johannesburg in three weeks' time. Bonnie traded a rain check on a future date with her motoring friend in exchange for the trunk call to Johannesburg which unsurprisingly confirmed his entry in the Nine Hour. While still on the phone to her friend, in a spur of the moment decision, she asked for her and Connie to be entered in the Lotus in the said race. She could have given no valid reason for this but in later discussion with Connie, it seemed to be a reasonable move to bring them closer to the South African if nothing else.

For two women to enter an extremely arduous and testing endurance race on another continent against an international field was on the face of it, irresponsible. This was not really so. Our intrepid pair had already competed twice in both the Le Mans 24-hour and the Mille Miglia and on each occasion came home in the minor placings.
Plans now had to be made for the proposed trip to sunnier climes in the other hemisphere. The last Operation Downfall had yielded another fund for current needs, even more than enough, to the delight of a beaming father O'Meara who was able to gratefully accept a cheque for five thousand pounds for immediate needs and a promise if not a guarantee, of the necessary hundred and fifty thousand pounds within the prescribed three months. He effusively blessed their project, as it had been briefly outlined to him, then their car and in true valedictory fashion, their dear darling selves.
Connie couldn't help but quip, "You pray for us and we'll prey on someone else for the sake of the orphanage"
The Lotus had left by air for Johannesburg two days before two warmly clad figures stood in the departure lounge of Heathrow airport. They had just over-weighed-in two large suitcases which contained masses of clothing climatically the opposite to what they now wore. Two toothpaste type smiles eliminated the need to pay extra for the overweight luggage.
Over the loudspeaker came:
"Will all passengers for flight SA 605 for Johannesburg please proceed to gate three."
Connie nudged her mate, started forward quoting: "Live fast, die young and have a good-looking corpse.

Chapter 4

The air-conditioned, pressurised cocoon slid through the dark skies. Inside the 747 and towards the rear, Bonnie and Connie sat back and relaxed as they traveled rapidly southwards. Fur coats had been removed and put on the luggage rack. Connie had the window seat of a block of three and spent much time gazing down from her window. The sea was not visible but occasionally lights could be seen from ships plying their slow trade routes. Sometimes a chiffon-like layer of cloud that passed below gave some idea of the height at which the aircraft flew.

Next to Bonnie in the aisle seat sat a middle-aged man with distinguished grey sideburns which matched his immaculate grey suit. He wasted little time in engaging the two women in conversation. He spoke in an Australian-like accent. He was, in his own words "pretty big in mining – gold, you know" and only too pleased to take them on a verbal tour of his city, Johannesburg. Bonnie and Connie were only too happy to listen to his oral flow and now and again one or the other would interject with a question regarding accommodation and the Kyalami racetrack.

Sterile dinners served on the inevitable plastic trays were made passable by a bottle of South African wine pressed on the girls by "Mr. Pretty Big". They were able to agree that it's quality surpassed that of many and equaled that of the better European wines. Eventually the mining magnet's voice ran down and sleep became the order of the moment. A refueling stop at Ilha do Sol was nothing more than a petty nuisance, since no passengers were allowed to disembark and indeed, if the truth be known few desired to do so.

It was only just light when, far below the plane, the blue of the sea gave way to a mosaic of browns and greys with only occasional greens of a vast country thirsting for the imminent rains. Signs of human habitation increased as they approached their destination which, when it presented itself, was unmistakable for the industrial smog that hung in an inversion layer over the variety of concrete blocks that was the city of Johannesburg, industrial heart of the Republic of South Africa. The airport lay some way from the city itself.

The chore of immigration and customs formalities was relatively painless and the two soon found themselves standing in the bright sun outside the terminal building, conscious of the thin air of the city situated at an unusually high altitude. They hailed a taxi and were impressed with the courtesy of the jolly, round, Bantu driver, who, contrary to prevailing custom in London, insisted on putting their luggage in the boot and opening the doors for his passengers.
Once seated in the taxi, Bonnie addressed the bar driver, "The Towers please".
"With pleasure Madams," came the reply as a taxi swung out of the airport complex onto a fast moving traffic covered freeway. On the way into the city, the driver like his white countrymen on the plane talked, mainly about himself, his ambitions and his plural wives and children. He spoke without rancor, but in what he said lay a semi-concealed indication of the unhappy state of race relations in that country.

*****

The Towers, recommended by "Mr. Pretty Big" proved to be a huge, modern and obviously expensive hotel right in the centre of the city. Here they paid off the taxi, adding a five Rand note towards the driver's myriad of children. The inside of the building was as imposing as the outside with so much marble and gilt as to be almost overwhelming. The accommodation provided on the 14th floor was sumptuously

comfortable, air-conditioned and en-suite with both bathroom and dressing room. Bonnie and Connie surveyed their surroundings.
"Not catering to the poor are they?" Connie asked rhetorically.
"I'm always ready for the hardships to be endured in the darkest continent" commented Bonnie.
Having declined the antiseptic morning offering on the plane, the two girls phoned room service for a slap-up breakfast which appeared within the space of a few minutes. After breakfast Bonnie called their shipping agents and arranged for the Lotus to be delivered to the hotel's underground garage. Both of the girls then took turns to bath and titivate themselves ready for their first sojourn into the new city. They both dressed in summer dresses of a similar design that clothed but did not over-conceal what they covered.

To find the Lotus not only undamaged after its journey but washed and polished, was an unexpected pleasure to its two owners. Even in the subdued light of the underground garage, the Lotus, in its red livery stood out amongst its fellows, mostly locally manufactured models of well-known Japanese and German makes. A one hundred percent duty on imported cars made exotic models rare, even in affluent and cosmopolitan Johannesburg. The sight of their car gave both the girls a feeling of security in a foreign land. Connie ran her hands appreciatively over the sleek bodywork and said:
"My girl, you're going to have to really prove yourself in two weeks' time against some heavy competition, especially one Porsche driven by one very nasty driver".
"She'll do it. What's a few horsepower between friends? Especially with such good hands at the wheel" added Bonnie with a wink at her companion.

The Lotus spiraled purringly upwards and onto the street. For their first morning in Johannesburg, the girls decided that, with the aid of a map thoughtfully provided by the shipping company and left on the dashboard, they would get to know the city and its environs before

settling down to practicing for the race and getting the car tuned. The need for the latter action was imperative as almost immediately they were aware that the high-powered engine of the Lotus was wrongly tuned for the rare atmosphere of the Transvaal Highveld. This raised a priority need, that of a garage or mechanic to prepare the car for the endurance race. The quest for this they decided to postpone until the following day.
They returned to their hotel shortly before sundown, exhausted from new sights and experiences and hungry, as all they had had since breakfast was a milkshake at a café in one of the suburbs. As they passed into the hotel foyer it was Bonnie who made a suggestion.
"Let's go out for a meal and sample a bit of nightlife, shall we?"
"I'm game, but not too late tonight. I'm bushed!" answered Connie
At the reception desk Bonnie asked the elderly Indian reception clerk, "Where is it all at?"
"I beg your pardon Madam?" came the reply.
"Don't be stuffy. Where's the best place to go for a night out?" said Bonnie.
"From my own experience, I wouldn't know but I believe for younger people like yourselves, they say that Hillbrow is the place Madame" came the pompous answer.
"And where's Hillbrow, my good man?" Connie had decided to match the Indian's pomposity. The Indian saw his mistake and thawed.
"Turn right outside the hotel entrance and just follow the street for a couple of kilometres and you can't miss all the lights and action. Please take care though, it is generally a pretty rough area. Have a good evening." He grinned and his grin widened as Bonnie passed him a folded ten rand note.
In their suite the two prepared themselves for their nocturnal sortie.
"Let's go Operation Downfall and shock the local yokels" said Bonnie referring to their slinky dresses.
"Yes let's. But no actual downfall, as I believe the authorities are a bit puritanical in this part of the world, okay?"
The locals might have been a bit puritanical in attitude but not to the

extent that they did not look at Bonnie and Connie in the lift with undisguised admiration.

*****

There was no missing high Hillbrow. It was alive and vibrant. Flickering and flashing neon lights, the odours of a hundred restaurants and the cacophony of noise that issued from the entrances of discos was exciting. Parking was a problem, but after circling a couple of blocks twice, Bonnie was able to smoothly ease the Lotus into a space just emptied by a departing car. The car had hardly come to a stop when a figure detached itself from the wall against which it had been leaning and walked across the pavement to stand in front of the locus Lotus. "Juslaaik!" said the large open faced, blonde haired young man, addressing nobody in particular. Bonnie and Connie heard the remark and were to a degree chagrinned when it became apparent that the foreign word of approbation was directed at the Lotus and not at their selves. They both got out of the car as a young man now addressed them directly.
"Man, that is some jammy you dolls got there."
Bonnie said to Connie, "I think this gorgeous hunk in the leather jacket is saying something nice about our car. I don't think he thinks much of its owners, do you?"
The young man smiled and went very red in the face, showing even through his appreciable tan.
"Hell man, I think you dolls are okay but you don't see a blik like that every day in Joeys.... sorry, I mean you are special'...... at least as much as your wheels....I....."
"You're making a mess of things aren't you? Why don't you just say that you're mad on cars and not girls?" laughed Connie.

The young man also laughed, "I'm Afrikaans, so I can't say things so well in English. You are a smart couple of chicks. I'm mad on cars. I must introduce myself, I am Jannie Els."
He stuck out a large hand to shake each of the girls hands
"Hello Jannie. We're Connie and Bonnie and are new in Johannesburg, from England." said Connie shaking hands.
"That's how come you got such a lekker car." observed Jannie.
"Yes, and what's more we have come to race it here in the Nine Hour Endurance Race in a couple of weeks' time." Replied Bonnie also shaking hands.
Jannie's eyes lit up, "Man, that's fantastic. I'm going to scrape together the money to go and watch even if I have to wash dishes. I'm a mechanic you know."
"You're joking" said Connie "Are you any good as a mechanic? We're going to need one."
"I could make that little baby of yours sing! He walked round the car and carried on, "This is a 1981 model with a 2.2 litre motor, 16 valve, mid-engine and with that blower can probably push close to 300 K's but maybe not on the Highveld. Oh! And by the way, in standard trim that motor pushes out 136 kW."

"Good grief! You certainly seem to know your cars Jannie!" came from a surprised Connie, "I'll tell you what, if you can mechanic a car as good as you can read Car Magazine, we'll give you a try as our mechanic if you can give us some of your spare time. I'm sure Bonnie will agree? We'll pay for your time, don't worry!"
Bonnie nodded in agreement.
Jannie stood openmouthed for a moment before saying, "You can have as much time as you like. I'm out of a job at the moment. I'll take standard hourly wages if that's okay with you?"
"Deal" said Connie, shaking hands again.
"Let's seal our bargain over dinner and a bit of dancing. You know the way around Hillbrow, so lead on Jannie."
Jannie looked embarrassed, "I haven't the bread to take you to eat out."

he said plaintively.
Bonnie laughed, "You got it all wrong. This is a business meal. We've got to get to know our new mechanic and so we pay."
Jannie guided the two girls along the crowded pavement. Drunks and other aggressive characters made way for them in the face of Jannie's bulk. The restaurant they ate at was Indian. They all tucked into an excellent Madras curry accompanied by vast amounts of fluffy rice and cooled their mouths with a succession of ice-cold lagers. To follow they sampled a variety of sweetmeats which in taste and odour, smacked of the exotic spices of the Orient. The lagers seem to lessen Jannie's initial shyness in the presence of the two Englishwomen. He told them of his family, his love of cars and his background. His state of unemployment was due to the fact that the garage which his father owned and in which he had learnt his trade and then worked, had gone bust. In the current recession small firms could not compete with a large companies.

The girls discussed the need for a garage where Jannie could work on the car, and also the need for accommodation at somewhat less than the exorbitant rates they were now paying at the hotel. Mechanic or no mechanic, Jannie earned his supper when he came up with a solution to both their problems. He had an aunt who owned a smallholding halfway between Johannesburg and Pretoria with a pleasant house and a large garage with an inspection pit and other equipment. She was away in Plettenberg Bay for three months and would, he was certain, be only too pleased to let the smallholding at a very reasonable rental if that suited them. It suited them and it was in a mood of happy accomplishment that they dragged a rather unwilling Jannie to a nearby disco.
"Nee man, I don't go for this type of jolling" he complained.
Nevertheless, it was a merry trio who walked out of the smoke laden, noise vibrant atmosphere of the disco into the street at two o'clock in the morning. Jannie politely saw the girls to the Lotus before driving off a bit erratically in his Daihatsu pickup. He had arranged to meet them that afternoon at the hotel and run them out to see his aunts place.
Bonnie and Connie had barely surfaced, showered, dressed and gulped

down some toast and black coffee, when Jannie arrived to collect them. He looked none the worse for wear after the nights carousing with his big smile and flashing blue eyes, as he led them to the hotel and out to his Daihatsu with an almost possessive air.
The smallholding was all that Jannie had said it would be. In fact, it was delightful. The house, in the old Cape Dutch style of architecture, stood on ten hectares of land and close below the house was a small dam on which a number of domestic ducks went about their business. The garage was spacious, more than large enough for their purpose and there were numerous outbuildings.
Jannie phoned his aunt from the house to confirm the tenancy for a period of two months at a rental which the girls thought was ridiculously low.

There being no reason for delay, it was agreed that they would check out the hotel the following day and settle into "Geluk", as the house on the smallholding was called. It seems sensible that Jannie should also join them but it took some time to break through his Calvinistic upbringing to get him to agree to such an apparently, immoral arrangement. Perhaps it was Bonnie's last effort at persuasion that worked.
"Listen Jannie even if I stick the bloody menu right under your nose, you don't have to order, do you?"
He finally agreed and this pleased the girls, as it would save time in that Jannie would not have to travel back and forth. Also, they would have him close by as guide and adviser, and at last but not least, as interpreter if required in a bilingual country.

The same Indian reception clerk seemed surprised when they announced their intention to cut short their stay. He could not resist the crack: "Perhaps the hotel is little too quiet for the ladies, not like Hillbrow !"
Connie looked up from checking their bill and replied, "Not at all. It's just that if we spent a couple of days longer here, it would've been cheaper to buy our own hotel!"

The Indian shrugged his shoulders and said nothing
Outside Jannie was waiting to take their luggage in his pickup. Happily, they set off for Geluk.

Chapter 5

Connie stood on the veranda and stretched. It was only seven in the morning but the air shimmered in a heat haze which promised an exceedingly hot day. The air was dry though compared to a hot summer's day in England and not unpleasant. From an outbuilding that stood semi-concealed in a small grove of gum trees, a mother duck made her ponderous way down to the dam. Her brood of six followed in single file. Connie was aware of metallic sounds coming from the garage which invited investigation.

The Lotus stood over the pit. From the rear protruded two track shoe shod feet. Jannie hummed tunelessly to himself, oblivious of his visitor.

"Morning, early bird!" called Connie.

Jannie extracted himself from the car. He grinned as he spoke.

"I woke early and couldn't keep my hands of this baby. You'll find she's okay for this altitude now. I've never worked on a Dell Orto carb before but I soon got the hang of it. Start up and just feel the difference."

Connie got into the driver's seat and started the engine. As Jannie had promised the engine ran smoother and was much more responsive when she depressed the accelerator. She got out and watched Jannie wiping his hands on a piece of rag.

"Scoff time, I scheme!" he said.

Connie's reply was to link arms and steer him back to the house. In their absence, Bonnie had risen and cooked a more than passable breakfast. Over coffee on the veranda they sat and planned their time until the day of the race. Short acquaintance or not, the two girls were impressed with Jannie and took a chance on telling him the whole reason for their being in South Africa and how they had entered the endurance race in the hope of getting close to van der Westhuizen. Trust in their new friend was well placed as Jannie did not hesitate to join them in their conspiracy against a man who not only killed a friend, Manny, but horror of all horrors, was a potential cause of the orphans losing their home. The girls realised the Jannie had a heart as big as his massive body and as soft as his body wasn't.

It was Bonnie who came up with a meritoriously outrageous way of getting van der Westhuizen into their clutches.
"How's this for a plan?. We are entered for the race, right? So is van der Westhuizen. His Porsche has the legs on the Lotus but if we push the Lotus and forget about completing nine hours we, at least whoever is driving, should be able to get alongside the Porsche and, at a predetermined corner, ease him off the track, it would be the last thing he would be expecting. Coming ......"
Connie interrupted. "You're kidding!"
"No" Bonnie continued "just listen! Coming off the track, van der Westhuizen will be at the very least shocked, if he rolls maybe even concussed. That's the moment to grab him."
"And how do we do that in front of thousands of spectators?" Asked Connie.
"No sweat," came from a face with an impish grin.
"Whoever is not driving, plus Jannie will be waiting near the scene of the accident with a dummy ambulance and dressed as paramedics. Before our friend can regain his wits, the paramedics jab him with some pentathol and cart him off in the ambulance as if he was injured. Then back here and van der Westhuizen can answer some leading questions!"
The other two gaped at the speaker.
"You're a genius!" said Connie in admiration.
"Man, that's a cheeky plan!" added Jannie.
"Jannie, you will help us won't you?" said the pouting originator of the plan.
"Ja, sure, and ....." Jannie looked exceedingly pleased with himself, "I can fix up an ambulance. All I need is a clapped-out van and my spray-painting outfit. Also, if two of us are busy snatching this chap, we'll need somebody in the pits. I know a couple of mechanics who would be pit crew just for the chance to be involved in motor racing. How's that?"
"Perfect" said Bonnie pecking Jannie on the cheek and producing another fit of blushing.
The plan as outlined seem good but to succeed needed intensive preparation. There was much to consider - a van to purchase and

disguise, uniforms to acquire and many other details be sorted out. The sun had reached its zenith by the time the three conspirators had decided what to do and how to go about it.

During the afternoon, Jannie pursued his love affair with the Lotus in the garage while Connie and Bonnie cleaned the house and went out in Jannie's Daihatsu to buy provisions to last a couple of weeks. Connie also rang the organiser of the endurance race to get details of arrangements for practice and official scrutiny of their car. He was very affable and offered to ring the security guards at the track to arrange the entry to the track at any time before the race.

At Jannie's insistence they had purchased among the provisions, boerewors and mutton chops and were delighted to be inducted that night, into the local ritual of the "braaivleis". Cooked over hot coals, the meat was delicious, the cold lager refreshing and the music from Jannie's mouth organ, though mainly monotonous Afrikaans folksongs, provided a relaxing and fitting end to their first day at Geluk.

*****

The following day was a hot and cloudless as the previous. By mid-morning Jannie pronounced the Lotus ready for practice. Having packed a picnic lunch, they set off to the track, the girls in the Lotus and Jannie and his tools in the Daihatsu. They entered Kyalami through the North gate from the West Rand/Pretoria Road. The stands and pits were deserted and the grass edging the black snake of tar was as yet uncut. They parked the Daihatsu in the shade at the pits. First Bonnie and then Connie took the Lotus round the 4.1 km track at a leisurely pace, discovering that the track was a fast one with a long straight of well over a kilometre. Three turns, two right-hand and one left hand were fast, two others were sharper and the S no tighter than many others they had raced through.

Once they were each reasonably accustomed to the track they pushed the speed up. They discovered that, coming out of the right-hander, the Kink, with full throttle, the car literally flew down the straight under the bridge and was clocking over 250 km/h prior to breaking for Crowthorne corner. Jannie insisted on joining each of the girls for a couple of laps. He sat seemingly unconcerned by the excessive speed and listened intently to the engine, happy with its tuning, suggesting that they retain the Goodyear tyres already on the car.

By four o'clock they'd all had enough for one day and sipped cold Coke in the pits. Connie and Bonnie were unanimous in choosing Sunset Bend as the proposed site for van der Westhuizen's takeout bid. It had the advantage that it was a slower corner than many of the others and, most important of all, there was a reasonably large expanse of grass on the outside of the bend meaning that spectators would be well away from the track and hopefully not able to reach van der Westhuizen before the bogus ambulance crew.
On leaving Kyalami the girls headed straight back to Geluk while Jannie made a detour to collect his spray-painting equipment.

*****

Again, the next day, Jannie went on his own, this time with two thousand rand in his pocket to purchase a van and suitable paint. On his return the girls found it difficult to share his enthusiasm for the apparent wreck of a VW Microbus he had purchased, even though it had only cost 600 Rand. Jannie, though, was not discouraged. For three days he ground, filled, buffed and spray-painted until he was satisfied and the girls were dumbfounded. Before them stood a real ambulance, perfect in every detail. Jannie proudly showed them that he had even remembered to

spray the letters of the word "ambulance" laterally inverted so that they would read correctly in the mirror of a car in front, as was the case with the genuine article.
"Jannie you're an artist!" cried Connie, her hands grasping his and dancing around him as he pivoted with her and revealed again his predisposition to redden in the face.
The next job tackled was the equipping of the ambulance inside to at least resemble the real thing at a distance. Jannie's ingenuity and craftsmanship knew no bounds. Wood and black plastic material became beds and steel piping in the same material became a stretcher. A fire extinguisher painted black with matching rubber tubing attached became a dummy oxygen supply unit. The two women were more than satisfied with their abduction vehicle.

Provision of suitable uniforms taxed Jannie's skills less than the ambulance. A visit to an army surplus store produced the uniforms and suitable headgear. The girls sewing ability, such as it was, helped to convert black cloth and cardboard into reasonable facsimiles of epaulettes. It having been decided that Connie would do the dirty work on the track, Bonnie tried on her uniform.
"Man, if I could be promised to be treated by a nurse like you, I'd be sick all the time!" said Jannie. All three laughed because in fact a slight miscalculation in the bust measurement of her uniform had converted Bonnie into a cross between Dolly Parton and Florence Nightingale.

The matter of getting hold of the pentathol and a syringe proved to be difficult and it was again a resourceful Jannie who came up with the answer, but only the day before the official race. He remembered a medical student who owed him one for getting a banger of a car into roadworthy condition. The student preferred to ask no questions and produced the goods.

Preparations were complete. Jannie even found time to get a spare tyres, fuel and certain spare parts for the Lotus and to also retune the car to his satisfaction. It was a relaxed and confident party that headed for Kyalami for official practice on the day before the actual race. Two mechanic friends of Jannie were waiting in the pits. They were obviously delighted with an official status at this, the South African Mecca of motor racing. Not one of our three had the heart to disillusion them by acquainting them with the fact that, if all went according to plan, their services would not be required.

The official scrutineers examined the Lotus and, having satisfied themselves that the car was unmodified and as standard a production car as they could ascertain, informed Connie and Bonnie that for handicap purposes they had been given a target time of 1 minute and 20 seconds per lap. Seeing that the drivers of the Lotus Elite entry had turned out to be two women, the officials were almost apologetic at expecting them to lap at an average speed of about 180 km/h. Bonnie and Connie were unperturbed, especially as they had no intention of maintaining such an average speed for the total nine hours.

For appearance sake both Connie and Bonnie took the Lotus round the track to be timed officially for a grid position on the following day. It was decided however, that Bonnie would not over exert herself but that Connie would do her best to get a decent position on the grid, hopefully within striking distance of van der Westhuizen's Porsche. Bonnie settled for a mediocre lap time of 1 min 16.2 seconds.

Connie had just pulled out of the pit lane onto the track for a last attempt at a better time when she saw a black Porsche quickly fill the mirror and then pass her. She recognised, by instinct rather than from the features largely hidden under a crash helmet, van der Westhuizen. Her blood boiled at this first sight of the man who had done so much to ones that she loved. She pushed hard down the straight through the gears in pursuit of the black Porsche. She took the Lotus nearly to the limit on every corner and was pleased to see that the distance between the two cars was not increasing perceptibly. For three laps she kept up the pressure and actually believed she had gained ground on the Porsche. Her face was white when she pulled into the pits.

"That's the bastard, the black Porsche!" She cried vehemently as she climbed out of the car.

"I think you're right, but he's done you a favour. He's pushed you to a time of 1 min 13.1 seconds." said Bonnie calmly.

Van der Westhuizen had indeed done her a favour. When the final grid positions were published in the late afternoon, the Lotus was on the second row of the grid right behind van der Westhuizen who had not surprisingly taken pole position.

Chapter 6

Race day dawned differently as if in recognition of the import of things to come. The sun hid behind the skeins of cirrus cloud and at ground level not a whisper of wind was apparent. The air hung like a wet blanket. Connie had not slept well, reduced to lying naked on her bed because of the high humidity. She had tossed and turned all night and now she sat on the veranda and welcomed the approach of daylight. She was tense, conscious of what she was to do on the track that day; aware that at the final moment she had to force van der Westhuizen off the track at a speed of about 140 km/h without killing herself or him for that matter.

She felt better when the others joined her. Jannie was unruffled as usual and after breakfast, packed spares and tools in the back of his pickup. With time still on his hands, he checked the Lotus again. Out of sight of the others he carefully added a measured amount of aviation spirit to the fuel cans of petrol for the Lotus and then filled the car's tank. He hoped that by raising the octane rating of the fuel it would give the Lotus a little extra speed but at the same time did not want Connie to race with the knowledge that she was racing illegally.

They arrived at the track in good time, Connie and the Lotus, Jannie and the pickup and Bonnie in the ambulance. Bonnie separated from the others just inside the Northgate and drove round the track to the opposite side to position the ambulance on the grass on the outside of Sunset Bend, far enough from the track for safety but near enough to have a head start on the spectators when the time came.

At the pits the two mechanics unloaded the Daihatsu and positioned fuel and spares ready for a pit stop. Connie sat on a pile of tyres and tried to relax. She was dressed in silver overalls and though she wore nothing underneath, was already sweating in the humid midday heat. Jannie fussed around, winding stopwatches, preparing pit signal boards and giving final instructions to the mechanics who were to deliver the signals in his absence which he explained would be necessary for the first hour or so as he had to return to the smallholding to fetch vital spares he had forgotten. The mechanics were too excited to question his somewhat peculiar proposed absence.

Fifteen minutes before the race was due to start, Connie pulled on a helmet and cotton gloves, climbed into the Lotus and cruised it slowly onto the starting grid. She was surrounded by Porsches but only had eyes for one, the black one in front of her. As the lights above them turned to green, forty-eight cars of varying capacity and capability roared off on the warm-up lap. As did the other drivers, Connie wove the Lotus from side to side to warm up the tyres. The cars returned to the grid and took up their positions. The starter gave the drivers their final instructions, stepped off the track and all eyes stared at the suspended light. Red changed to green and with an ear shattering roar from about four thousand kilowatts worth of engines, the cars sped off down the straight, jostling for position before Crowthorne Corner. For fear of getting involved in a smash in the first frenzied seconds of the race, Connie did not insist on a right-of-way with too much emphasis and found that coming out of Barbecue Bend, the second corner, she was lying sixth behind five Porsches and a Maserati Bi-turbo. The black Porsche was in front.

She took a tight inside line through the fast left-hander, Jukskei Sweep and passed the Maserati. For the rest of the circuit she decided to tuck in behind the fifth Porsche, knowing that the drivers in front of her would, after a couple of laps, accept their relative positions and tap off just enough to ensure their cars lasted the next nine hours.

The Lotus was running like it had never run before and with the tow she got down the straight in the slipstream of the red Porsche in front, Connie had to consciously reduce pressure on the accelerator to avoid running into it. As she had expected the pace slackened perceptibly. By

the third lap she decided to start improving her position. Again, she chose Jukskei Sweep to pass and shot past on the inside of the red Porsche. There were now three cars between her and that of van der Westhuizen.
The distance between the Lotus and the Porsche lying fourth rapidly diminished as she pushed hard through the esses and Leeukop bend. Again, she got a tow down the straight. This time she watched the brake markers carefully and using four powerful disc brakes, outbreaked the next Porsche to enter Crowthorne corner a car length ahead and able to choose her line through the corner and force a startled driver to take a slower line on the outside of the bend. She had seen the red helmeted driver shake his head as she passed him.

'Two down and three to go,' she thought as she flashed past the pits.
On the long straights she had time to sit back for a few seconds and glanced to her right. Her pit signal board was being held up with the information regarding her position which she knew, plus the encouraging news that she had just lapped in 1 min and 13 seconds. What she was not aware of was that loudspeakers were broadcasting the fact that entry number twenty-seven had just broken the lap record for its class.

It only took Connie two laps to pass two more Porsches and two more bewildered drivers. Connie grinned as she thought "you poor male chauvinists would have a thrombie if you knew it was a woman that had just passed you".
Van der Westhuizen was now about two hundred metres in front of her and the slow traffic of the cars that were being lapped was making it difficult to reduce the distance. Connie was fast around most of the track as she used the corners to her advantage but there was no way she could match van der Westhuizen's 300 km/h down the straight.

Meanwhile in the opening laps of the race, Jannie had left the pits in the Daihatsu and headed across the track to the other side. Here he went

under the track via the subway and found a parking place amongst the spectators cars not far from the innocent looking ambulance. He ambled over and when he was sure no one was observing, climbed in next to Bonnie.
"How is Connie doing?" she asked.
"Man, she's driving like the devil. She will be up with van der Westhuizen within the first half-hour." he replied
With this he climbed into the back of the ambulance and dressed in his uniform.

Back on the track, Connie was having her work cut out to reduce the distance between herself and the black Porsche. On one lap she went through clubhouse corner too fast and, in an adrenaline producing detour off the track, lost a couple of precious seconds. Perhaps the adrenaline helped, because she now took the Lotus to the limit on every corner and by the twenty fourth lap was on van der Westhuizen's tail through the Kink. This time he didn't pull away down the straight. By keeping her foot flat in fifth year and using his slipstream, she stayed with him. Now she was able to hold the Lotus only a couple of metres behind the Porsche.
"Now you sod, shake me off if you can!' she thought to herself.
Van der Westhuizen must've been reading her thoughts, because she saw him glance worriedly into his mirror on a number of occasions.

For four laps, she stuck behind her quarry and worried him. Proof that she was making her presence felt came in the form of a couple of trips that the Porsche made half, but not completely off the track at Clubhouse Bend. With an iron will Connie stayed with him and watched carefully the line he took through Sunset. He was taking too tight a line through the corner for her to edge into the inside and force him off.

"Okay, we'll have to make you change your line." She said to herself.
She didn't hear the announcement of another new, class lap record as she shot down the straight for the thirtieth time. She braked slightly

later than van der Westhuizen at Crowthorne and was now a dangerous single metre behind the Porsche. Holding the position all through Barbecue and Jukskei, at the approach to Sunset, she did it! She braked very late and hit the Porsche hard on his right rear bumper with the Lotus's left front bumper. Van der Westhuizen got such a fright that he swerved marginally left. Connie dropped a gear and was into the gap on his inside. Out of the corner of her eye she saw his worried face as he struggled with the steering wheel. She let the Lotus go wide and van der Westhuizen had no option but to leave the track in a cloud of dust. Connie too, could not hold the Lotus and it shot onto the grass, but at a shallower angle than the Porsche. Van der Westhuizen's trip into the bush had not been in one sitting position, as the screaming tyres cut sideways through the dry grass, then momentarily gripped enough to arrest the sideways motion of the car, causing it to flip onto its roof and then back onto its wheels.

Bonnie and Jannie had been expecting what happened for at least four laps and were ready. Before the Porsche had stopped moving they were out of the ambulance and running towards the vehicle. Jannie carried the stretcher and Bonnie the medical bag. They reached the Porsche to find van der Westhuizen sitting dazed, not even attempting to remove the seatbelt. Jannie reached through the shattered window and grabbed an arm which he pulled out to hang down outside the driver's door. In this position he firmly held it while Bonnie removed an already charged syringe from the black bag and swiftly injected the sodium pentathol into a vein in the arm from which Jannie had violently torn the sleeve. Van der Westhuizen's head lolled to one side and his eyes closed. A shaken Connie climbed out of the damaged Lotus and walked across to the Porsche, reaching it at the same time as a worried track marshal and the first of the spectators. Ignoring Connie and the marshal, the other two quickly removed the unconscious man from the car and placed him on the stretcher.

Bonnie said for the sake of the spectators who now crowded around:

"Probably concussed, but we'll take him to the General for a checkup."
A paunchy gentleman tried to insist on helping Jannie with the stretcher, but Bonnie brushed him aside and took one end of the stretcher.

Connie now saw the danger of the crowd following the stretcher and getting too close and able to look at the inside of the ambulance. She yelled "Fire!" loudly and ran towards the Lotus. The crowd followed and by the time Connie had apologised for the false alarm, the ambulance had gone and so had Jannie's pickup. Some of the crowd round the Lotus were abusive, accusing Connie of dangerous driving. She ignored the abuse, got into the car and returned to the track and drove at a relatively sedate speed back to the pits. Her mechanics were disappointed but understood her desire to retire after such a shattering experience. She asked them to take charge of the spares, fuel and tyres, and then gave them each two hundred rand and left Kyalami.

*****

Shadows were starting to lengthen as Connie drove up to the house. Bonnie and Jannie waited on the veranda, looking extremely pleased with themselves. There was no sign of the ambulance or the uniforms.
"Where is he?" she demanded.
"Safe and sound in the shed over there." said Bonnie pointing to a windowless building made of stone and with an old but substantial door of roughhewn planks.
"Do you want our friend to talk now?" asked Jannie, clenching and unclenching a very large fist.
"He'll keep a bit and I need a shower and a drink first." said Connie, climbing the veranda steps and disappearing into the relatively cool interior of the house. An hour later, Jannie escorted a shaken van der Westhuizen through the dusk to the lighted house. He made no attempt to escape, partly because he was still groggy from the drug and partly

because of the wooden batten that his captor carried in one hand. The two women examined the man that they had traveled halfway round the world to meet. He was tall, well-built and about forty years old. The cruel lines of his mouth were accentuated by a narrow moustache which outlined his upper lip.
He blasted "What the hell do you think you're doing? A maniac damn near kills me at Kyalami and then you lot kidnap me!"
Connie replied sweetly "I'm the maniac and you have been kidnapped because we have some questions to ask you."
"I don't know you and I have nothing to say to you." spat out van der Westhuizen.
"Oh, I think you have!" Bonnie walked up close to him and stared at him, "You killed a friend of ours, Manny Cohen, and what's more, when you swindled him over the emeralds, you placed the home of a lot of innocent children in jeopardy!"
"I don't know what you're talking about!"
Jannie's fist seemed to bury itself in his midriff and he collapsed into a heap, only to rise immediately as Jannie grabbed his head and raised his arm into a horizontal position. Jannie released his hold on the hair and hit him again, this time with his knee in the groin. Van der Westhuizen lay on the veranda floor in a groaning heap. "We want two things from you." said Bonnie grimly, "We want a signed confession from you, admitting that you killed Manny and we want the money back."
"Go to hell, you bitch!" came the muffled reply from van der Westhuizen's bowed head.
Half an hour later van der Westhuizen was a mess but an accommodating mess. Most of his teeth lay on the veranda floor, one eye was almost closed and his bare torso bore livid marks from the wooden batten.
"I'll talk!" he said through bubbles of blood. What he had to say however convinced Connie and Bonnie that their problems were only partly solved. Van der Westhuizen admitted to killing Manny but not at his own instigation. He was not the principal but the servant. He had been ordered to dispose of Manny Cohen. Furthermore, he was not the owner

of the emeralds but only the salesman. Words continue to flow from the damaged mouth as he kept an eye on the bloody batten that Jannie still held. The owner of the emeralds, the miner of the genuine emeralds, the manufacturer of the synthetic emeralds and the architect of the deceit and violence in which the girls were now caught up, was Hartley de Vere Courtney, currently resident of Zimbabwe and owner of the Duiker mine near Shurugwe.

Chapter 7

The land they flew over was a little changing, sleeping giant. One hundred million years might have altered a river course fractionally and worn away a few centimetres of granite kopje tops but little else had changed except the people whose national spirit had been recently aroused and pitched helter-skelter into burgeoning statehood, the new Zimbabwe. The plane they flew in belonged to the national air carrier and was a veteran of many years of aerial commuting. The flight crew were, however, friendly and the flight itself mercifully short.

Behind lay Geluk where Jannie had been left to guard the broken van der Westhuizen. A decision as to what to do with the self-confessed killer was to be postponed until Courtney had been approached. A captive van der Westhuizen could well be useful as a bargaining point.

Below the plane, Kipling's greasy Limpopo river ran and ahead, a confrontation with one who, by the admission of his emerald salesman, was barely qualified to bear the title "human". Connie and Bonnie sat back and enjoyed the rugged scene below but not the pilots frequent diversions round approaching thunderheads. The "fasten seatbelt" sign stayed on for the duration of the journey.

The main runway ran next to an agricultural experimental station whose trial plots of tobacco intrigued one by their regularity. The tarmac was wet, mute witness to one of the frequent tropical showers characteristic of this time of the year. Progress through customs and excise was slow, as the official involved, though polite, was insistent that regulations and procedures be strictly adhered to.

One trolley sufficed for the luggage and led the way through the main concourse and onto the steps outside the terminal building.
A voice said, "Good afternoon your Honours." It came from a black child of about eleven years of age and dressed in impeccable rags.

"Afternoon yourself, Huckleberry." returned Bonnie.
The boy looked confused "I am not Hucklebelly. I am Lucky!" he said, continuing with, "I am your first-class tour guide and servant!"
"Is that so?" queried Connie
"Yes, so. For two dollars a day I work for you and three dollars for Saturday. On Sunday I rest!" declared lucky.
His brave words were not matched by the hopeful, almost pleading look in his eyes. This was obvious to the two women and prompted Bonnie to say: "We'll give you a try. How's that?" Lucky's eyes widened and a huge grin took the place of verbal assent. He took the handle of the trolley firmly and steered it to a waiting taxi. Reveling in this importance, he ordered the driver to place the cases in the boot. When Connie and Bonnie were ensconced in the backseat of the taxi, Lucky climbed into the front seat beside the driver. The driver requested a destination.
"Monomatapa," was promptly ordered by Lucky and the girls were content to leave it to their little man of the world. They had intended to stay at the Monomatapa Hotel anyway. The airport lay some miles out of the city and the drive produced an interesting series of scenes of the living conditions of the "haves" and "have-nots". The Monomatapa Hotel in Samora Machel Avenue was large and modern, though of pre-independence vintage.

The reception clerk at the decks was apologetic. The hotel was full. Lucky whispered to Connie who promptly gave him four ten-dollar notes. Lucky pocketed one and handed the other three to the clerk. No progress was made until Lucky launched into a verbal barrage of Shona. Suddenly the receptionist nodded his head violently and turned to get a key from a hook on the wall behind them. He placed a key on the counter and full of smiles indicated the need to sign the register. He explained his change of heart.
"I'm sorry madams. We always keep a couple of our best rooms available for such important visitors as yourselves."
Lucky accompanied the luggage into the lift.

"What the hell do you tell the chap at the desk?" Bonnie demanded
Guileless eyes looked at her, "I told him you were members of a mission coming here to arrange loans for country." He hurried on, "it was not really a lie. You might be what I said, I don't know."
The girls laughed delightedly at his ingenuity.

The room was pleasant and overlooked a park that backed on to the hotel. Lucky examined the room and pronounced it acceptable. He then took over the chore of tipping the porter to his own benefit, a dollar for the porter and another one for himself. The girls were enchanted with the pocket size rogue.
"What you want now?" demanded Lucky.
"Nothing more today, little man. We are going to relax and have an early night. Tomorrow you can help us to find wheels for our stay here... hire a car or something. By the way we will need to go to a mine near Shurugwe, so make sure you get us directions. That's all, I think." replied Bonnie.

Lucky took his leave with a promise to be in attendance at eight the following morning. Connie and Bonnie unpacked and then showered and dressed. By the time the two had finished it was time to join the hundreds of escapees from workplace prisons who crowded the bars downstairs. The drinkers were a very cosmopolitan crowd and a dozen languages from at least three continents were discernible. Though the sun was well set, it was hot in the bar and the girls drank the local beer, well iced. A couple of the local whites made passes at the women but got nowhere. Sweaty brows, penduline paunches did not appeal to them on their first night in Harare.

Dinner was taken in the Bali Hi restaurant and at the conclusion of the meal, they were forced to admit that the Nasi Goring was as good as they had had on the Plein in Amsterdam. Back in their room before nine o'clock, they settled down for the night. With windows wide open, they were dreamily aware of the high-pitched cicada concert from the park below their window.

*****

Lucky, considerably spruced up, was waiting outside the hotel room before seven. He had an hour to wait before Connie and Bonnie put in an appearance. They had used room service for breakfast.
"Right, Lucky my boy. First thing this morning, is to organise wheels." said Connie as they stepped towards the lift.
"Madam, I have made a plan for you. If you hire a car, it will cost you a lot of money. I have an uncle who sells cars. I've talked to him and he says he will lend you a car from his garage for a small payment. No worry about insurance and license. You like?"
"We like, you wheeling and dealing little devil!!" laughed Connie

Outside the hotel, Lucky instructed his charges to follow him, an action they regretted as it took them the best part of an half hour's walking before they reached "Sam Chiweshe's Cars" in one of Harare's backstreets. Lucky made introductions. Sam Chiweshe was large, very black and jovial. He showed them his stock which consisted of four cars in various stages of decrepitude and a Land Rover in what appeared to be reasonable condition. Not wishing to hurt Lucky's feelings or his pocket, Connie and Bonnie made the obvious choice. Ten minutes later, two hundred dollars poorer and the Land Rover turned out of the used-car lot onto the street, Connie driving. Sam's hire charge for an initial ten days was in fact cheap.

The jacaranda and flamboyant trees for which Harare is rightfully renowned were in full bloom and under Lucky's direction the Land Rover made a fairly comprehensive tour of the city and its suburbs. The only stop they made was at a suburban stationers, where they purchased a book containing large-scale maps of Zimbabwe. Back at the hotel the girls persuaded a reluctant Lucky to join them for lunch. They felt that his meager frame looked as if it was in need of a square meal. Lucky's manners were surprisingly good for a street urchin and it was only between mouthfuls that his story came out.

He was the oldest of four children which his mother battled to raise in a shanty at Mufakose on the outskirts of Harare, her husband having been killed during the war of independence. His mother took in washing and Lucky, actually fifteen years old, found work where and when he could. He admitted that when times were really bad he had to resort to theft, something he was not proud of.

After lunch Bonnie paid Lucky for the two days and not needing him again that day, arranged for him to come to the hotel at eight o'clock the following morning.

From the room, Bonnie rang reception and asked for a call to be placed to Courtney at Shurugwe. Within a few minutes she was through. The voice that answered the phone sent shivers down her spine.
"Hartley DeVere Courtney speaking." said an oily, high-pitched but cultured voice.
"Mr. Courtney, you don't know me, my name is Boncherie Armatrading. I'm from London and my friend Miss Bojangles and myself have some business we wish to discuss with you."
"My dear lady, you're quite right, I don't know you. What business could you possibly have with me?" came the disgusting voice at the other end of the line.
"Mr. Courtney. I think you should see us. We have important business involving emeralds and a dead customer of yours, Manny Cohen." Bonnie insisted.
There was a pause before he answered.
"Perhaps Madam, the conversation would be better continued face-to-face and not on the telephone. I shall expect you for tea at three thirty tomorrow. You do take tea, don't you? Directions to my little kingdom

you can get by asking anybody when you reach Shurugwe."
Before Connie could agree or disagree, Courtney had rung off. Bonnie turned to Connie and shrugged.
"Yuck! He sounds as queer as a three-pound note."
"Bugger what his sexual preference is, we want the money. I'll drink river water, never mind tea as long as we get that!" replied Connie.

Examination of the appropriate map in the book they had bought showed the village of Shurugwe about half an hour's drive from Gwelo, a city about three hours' drive from Harare. Allowing say, half an hour to get to the mine it meant that they had best leave Harare about ten thirty or eleven and have lunch somewhere on the way.

The rest of the afternoon, they occupied pleasantly by taking a drive out to see Mazoe Dam an easy thirty minutes' drive from Harare. They were impressed with the rich farmland that they drove through and also with the mineral-rich dyke on the way to the dam. At the dam, women and children stood knee deep in the water and fished with reel-less rods made of thin branches, nylon line and corks. Every time a cork bobbed, the angler struck and nine times out of ten sent a miniature bream flashing through the air to land on the bank behind. Here, as quick as lightning, a mere toddler deftly removed the fish from the hook, checked the bait and signaled the angler to flick the line back into the water. Connie and Bonnie marvelled that the locals were more than happy to fish for piscine specimens at which any self-respecting English cat would turn up its nose.

On the way back from Mazoe Dam they were caught in a thunderstorm and cursed Sam Chiweshe when they discovered that there was no hood for the Land Rover. Ignoring the funny looks they got as they dripped their way through the foyer of the hotel, the first thing they did when they reach their room was to ring room service and order a bottle of brandy.
"I love living rough," sighed Connie as she lay back in the steaming bath

and sipped at the half tumbler full of brandy.
"Bonnie" she continued, "we've got an unpleasant day ahead of us tomorrow. Let's get our mind off Courtney by going to a nightclub and sampling the nightlife of Zimbabwe."
"Perfect idea. Perhaps we will get picked up by a big, bronzed mercenary and marched off to his bed at gunpoint." giggled Bonnie.
"You wish!" retorted Connie.

At nine that night it was a different pair who passed through the foyer of the hotel again. This time the looks were anything but funny. The simple cotton dresses they wore stunned by their subtle brevity and body clinging lines.

"The Kraal" nightclub was only two blocks away, so they walked. The décor of the club was dreadful, perhaps best described as "modern tribal", judging by the garish and obviously imitation masks, shields and spears which adorned the walls. The cover charge was sheer robbery but the girls paid up and took their places on two stools at the bar. Their eyes swept the room which was dimly lit by a couple of red bulbs mounted behind masks on the wall. At one end of the room was a small, slightly better lit stage on which a tired band of four black musicians played a succession of out of date Western tunes with a beat intended to sound ethnic. The smoke haze that hung everywhere was sweetly laced with a fair dollop of what Connie and Bonnie recognized as marijuana.

Four tunes, during which a few couples gyrated about the minuscule dance floor, then the band woke up long enough to give a loud introduction to the resident stripper. She was black and in a tremendous hurry to get out of her clothes and off the stage. She was a great hit with the locals but to the English girls, she appeared to be suffering from a severe case of stygiopia, so large was her backside. The feather boa she swept back and forth in a vain attempt to conceal the most private part of the body added colour to the scene by shedding its feathers on the nearest of the spectators. At one stage, she lowered herself sexily into a sitting position on one of the patrons' tables only to shoot upright with a yell as her bottom make contact with a lit cigarette in an unnoticed ashtray. It was a relief when eventually she fled, quite quickly for her size, from the stage. By this time the band had disappeared and onto the stage stepped a man dressed in jeans and a denim shirt. He carried a guitar and took his time taking a seat in the spotlight. Though his hair was steel grey and his face lined, his body was that of a younger man, barely thickened at the waist.

He pulled the microphone towards him and without a smile to the audience, started to sing. He sang first in English and then in Shona. The songs he sang had never been heard by the girls before. They were sad songs, everyone without exception, about war and the aftermath of war. When he finished a song in English, the whites in the audience clapped and shouted and after each Shona song the blacks in the audience gave him the same degree of appreciation.
A voice at Connie's shoulder said pleasantly in a cultured tone: "A man for all seasons."
Connie half turned to face the speaker seated next to her. He was an impeccably dressed black officer of the Zimbabwean army, a full colonel to boot.
"How'd you mean?" asked Connie
"Listen to the audiences reaction. He sings for the whites about the Selous Scouts and the farmers who fought the terrorists. Then he sings sad songs about the freedom fighters who went overseas for military training, of the wives and children who lost their husbands and fathers in the fight for independence. Indeed, a man for all seasons yet a sad man. He was a soldier of no mean repute."
"Who is he?" asked Connie now intrigued.
"He is Captain Michael John Dunne, formerly of the Selous Scouts. In his day he was probably the one man, we, the freedom fighters feared the most. You know why we feared him. Well, I'll tell you. It was because he was a black man in a white man's skin. He thought like us and pre-

empted us every time. He was also fearless and totally dedicated to what he was doing, hunting us down. Yes, if there had been many more like him, we might never have won the war."
"Why is he singing in a nightclub then, if he is such a good soldier? Why isn't he in the same uniform as you," asked Bonnie, who had heard most of the conversation.
"Simply because he was a Selous Scout." stated the black officer as if it explained everything.
"It seems a shame though." said Connie, her eyes back on the figure on the stage who was taking large gulps of some spirit from a glass, as he paused between songs.
"It is sad," sighed the colonel, "look at him. A wreck of a man, ravaged by alcohol, a soldier who must seek out a living in a dump like this. He is tolerated by us blacks because he sings songs. He's lucky there because virtually all of the Scouts had to flee the country before independence. Believe it or not, I respect him and even call him Captain."

The subject of the conversation at the bar, had sung his last song. He stood up, guitar in one hand, briefly acknowledged the applause and made his slightly unsteady way off the stage.

For another hour or so Connie and Bonnie talked to the colonel who proved to be intelligent and erudite. He talked about his country and the "bush war" with a surprising lack of rancor. He did not ask either of the girls to dance but at the same time his presence discouraged other potential dancing partners. He insisted on paying for the drinks and finally on escorting the two back to the Monomatapa, where he left them with a smart salute and gentle goodbye

*****

Chapter 8

Bonnie could have cried. A mere five hours after hitting the sack she was forcibly woken by the noise that drifted up from the park. She got up and looked out of the window. Below her a violent verbal interchange ensued between two large and vocally equally matched black viragos. A crowd gathered and a light-hearted cheering for the two women added to Bonnie's discomfort. She gave up hope of getting back to sleep, so read the previous day's paper until the morning tea arrived at seven.

The girls dressed for traveling comfort, in jeans and T-shirts, which clung deliciously to their bra-less breasts. Lucky arrived just as they finished breakfast in their room. They explained to him that his services would not be required that day but that he would be paid all the same. Far from being pleased at being paid for doing nothing, Lucky looked crestfallen. They were not prepared to take him with them, especially as there was a chance that Courtney might turn nasty. They felt capable of taking care of themselves but not a third party.

It was just before 11 o'clock as the Land Rover set off along Samora Machel Avenue. Within ten minutes they were clear of the city and bowling along at a steady hundred kilometres an hour, at which speed the heavily treaded tyres hummed on the tarmac, not unpleasantly. The road gradually swung towards the south-west as it passed over the succession open msasa tree covered hills.

Selous was nothing more than a few shops and Kadoma, the next town, still not a metropolis of any size. The town of Kwekwe seemed well-placed for lunch and it was just on one o'clock that the Land Rover swung into a parking place, blue carpeted with flowers fallen from the jacaranda trees.

Back on the road, it took less than an hour to Gweru, the largest town in the central region of Zimbabwe. Instead of continuing on the main road to Bulawayo, they swung Southeast, following the signs to Shurugwe, a small town owing its existence to the district's farming and mining activities and its fame to its being the hometown of the former, rebel Prime Minister of the then Rhodesia, Ian Smith. They filled the tank at the garage and at the same time asked directions to the Duiker Mine. The petrol attendant gave them a very searching look and then in a tone of voice bordering on the surly told them to take the first left turn just out of the town and to follow the dirt road for about fifteen kilometres. When they reached the mine they would know, he ended with a smirk.

It had not rained in the area for a couple of days and the dust from the dirt road in the open vehicle was stifling. It was especially bad when they slowed through bends, as there was a strong tail wind blowing which at times exceeded the speed of the moving vehicle. They could not have missed the Duiker Mine. Next to the signboard was a substantial diamond mesh wire gate, closed and locked. Attached to either side of the gate and stretching as far as the eye could see was a fence of the same material with an additional four angled strands of barbed wire.

The Land Rover stopped at the gate and Bonnie, who was driving, hooted. A figure in a uniform of drab olive material sauntered from a building near the gate. He stopped before he reached the vehicle, turned and returned to the building. After a few minutes Bonnie got impatient and hooted again. This time the uniform figure unlocked the gates and without a word, waved them through. They now passed along an avenue of gum trees which seemed to stretch in a straight line towards the rock-strewn hills.

As the trees flashed by, the girls could see, standing well back from the road, a succession of small houses all exactly the same and each with a singular lack of garden. Nearer to the hill the small houses gave way to open ground. Just below the hill a long, low building with barred windows was visible. It looked like a barracks. The more so for the several uniformed figures who lounged about on the bare sunbaked

earth in front of the building. At the base of the hill the road started to turn and climbed a full circle before it had reached the top a good hundred and fifty metres above the plane. Bonnie brought the Land Rover to a stop before a set of massive stone steps which led up to a house, or more correctly, a stone mansion that stood three-storied in foreboding silence, between massive granite boulders greater and higher than the building itself. On the patio between the top step and the house itself was a gold painted wrought iron garden suite. From one of the chairs, a flabby mountain of a man raised himself. His head was hairless as was his face and jowls hung down over the collar of his shirt. He was dressed in a cream seersucker suit of dimensions which would have taxed the ingenuity of a reputable tent maker.
Connie and Bonnie shook the dust from their clothes and side-by-side climbed the steps. Courtney met them at the top with: "Pleased to meet you my dears. My gate guard phoned to say you are on your way. I hope you had a pleasant journey."

With this he extended the soft, white flaccid hand that dripped gold rings and whose nails were immaculately manicured. One woman and then the other declined to accept the handshake. Courtney seemed unperturbed, for he sniggered and said: "As you wish, you plebeians! I have no real wish to make physical contact with your kind anyhow. But I forget my manners! Let us take a seat on the patio and partake of some tea. So refreshing in the heat, I always think. Then perhaps you can tell me why you are here."

He led the way to the mosaic topped table from which he picked up a small bell and tinkled gently. All three sat down with their backs to the house, facing out over the plain that seemed to extend from below them to the horizon.

A door opened behind them and two young blacks, about twenty years old and clearly identical twins, appeared and silently stood in front of Courtney. They were similarly attired in gold sandals, gold running

shorts and string vests of the same hue. The vests scarcely concealed the perfectly defined muscles rippling underneath. Physically they were magnificent.
"May I present Adonis and Narcissus, my young shadows." said Courtney. He addressed the two young men.
"Darlings, please rustle us up a pot of the Earl Grey and some of those delectable Cadbury's chocolate biscuits."
The two nodded and departed.

In their absence Courtney felt obliged to explain.
"Beautiful aren't they? Belong to me – literally! In this country it is considered exceedingly unlucky to produce twins and up until not long ago it was the custom to put them to death immediately after birth. I paid their mother handsomely and removed from her the obligation of dispensing with them. I had them wet-nursed, raised and educated them myself and now they belong to me, body and soul."
Connie and Bonnie were too disgusted to make comment.

Adonis and Narcissus returned with a solid silver tea service and Royal Doulton cups. In keeping with the totally unreal situation, the sugar was in lump form with accompanying tongs. All that was missing was a butler to pour the tea. Instead, Courtney did the honours whilst his two young blacks took up positions behind his chair.

Courtney gazed out across the plain and indicated with his hands. "I want you to consider my little kingdom here before we get down to business. In that way you may appreciate, or at least understand any stance I may take in our discussions. If you look carefully you may able to see the firebreak which indicates the position of the fence around my property. Even if you can't, let me tell you that I own twenty thousand prime acres of land. Behind this hill there is a mine which continues to yield gem quality emeralds. Behind ......"
Connie interrupted, "aren't you forgetting the laboratory where you manufacture the synthetic emeralds?"

"Ah, yes, I see you know about them! They are however, synthesized in my plant behind the house. Yes, the house behind us, I was about to tell you, contains what is probably the finest private collection of paintings and objects d'art in Southern Africa. All this I have created from nothing." He paused and then, before either girl could comment, continued,
"I came from nothing, my mother deserted me at birth. I've hated her and her gender ever since. My father did his best but died a pauper on me. I determined at the age of ten that come hell or high water, I would become fabulously rich and therefore protect myself from the buffets of this cruel world we live in. I achieved my aim but now I have tired of the crudity of Africa and wish to uproot and settle with my two beauties, to enjoy the last portion of my allotted span in the more comfortable and cultural surroundings of Switzerland. So, I have bared my soul. Now you state your business."

It was Connie who did the talking, "Mr. Courtney! I use the word Mister loosely. We are friends of Manny who you duped out of two million pounds and then had killed. No don't bother to deny it! Van der Westhuizen has confessed and he is right at this moment our prisoner in South Africa. When the time comes we will hand him over to the authorities. In the meanwhile, we want from you, Manny Cohen's money plus some extra, by way of reparation. Understand! We need the money to clear a mortgage on an orphanage, or else the kids go homeless."

She paused and Courtney spoke, "Your story touches me. The money you won't have simply because it buys my escape to Europe. I worked hard to build up my stake outside this cursed and currency exchange regulation bound country and you can both just forget about it. As regards van der Westhuizen, his babblings which I admit have a semblance of truth about them, worry me not one jot. You are forgetting that relations between South Africa and Zimbabwe are pretty sour and there is no extradition treaty between them!

Connie rose from her chair and made towards Courtney, "You bastard of the first water! You terrestrial Moby Dick! you'll come across ......!" Courtney shrilled, "Adonis, Narcissus! And Connie froze as she saw the Walther P38's that had appeared as if by magic in the respective left hands of both Adonis and Narcissus, one each pointed at her and Bonnie's heads.

"I hate violence but you have forced my hand. You two know too much. You will have to be eliminated: tomorrow morning shall we say? Please follow me!"

At gunpoint Connie and Bonnie followed Courtney as he waddled through the two huge carved doors that lead into the house. They saw that Courtney had not exaggerated. Each room they passed through was a veritable treasure house of antique furniture, valuable Persian rugs and recognizable art masterpieces. From the back door of the house, Courtney crossed a courtyard to an outhouse whose door he flung open to reveal a bare windowless room. Adonis and Narcissus pushed the two women inside and they heard the door shut solidly behind them.

A little light penetrated the room from beneath the door to reduce the almost complete darkness to a gloom that showed that this placed was empty of anything but themselves. Bonnie tried the door without success. It was solid and either locked or barred on the outside. By the dull rattling sound heard when she pushed against the door, she mentally opted for a bar and not a lock.

Connie peered through the semidarkness at her companion and said mournfully, "a right bloody mess we're in now! I don't see any way out."
"It looks like it," said Bonnie who had by this time examined the floor and each wall for anything that might aid in an attempt to escape. They both sank down on their haunches to more comfortably pass away time which, in a darkened state, they were not accurately aware of.
"It looks to me," said a doleful Connie, "that we will get nothing out of

Courtney except by force."
"Sure, agreed Bonnie, and what the hell is the use of two female karate black belts against a man with his two black poofters, always ready to stick the barrel of a P38 down your gullet if you so much as blink an eyelid."
"We must fight fire with fire. That's assuming we ever get out of this black hole of Calcutta." mused Connie. "Assuming we get out of here alive, we have to come back armed and preferably with reinforcements. I doubt the authorities will help us, so we will have to do it alone, I was wondering about that man in the nightclub. The colonel said he was one hell of a soldier. Maybe he could help us and ....."
Bonnie interrupted, "you're joking of course! That alcoholic can barely wield a guitar never mind a firearm!"
"I think you're wrong, Bonnie. Once a fighter always a fighter. We could give him a crash rehabilitation course, assuming he would agree and then come back here with our six guns blazing, that's if we get out of this place."
" Okay. We'll give him a try, if and when." Conceded Bonnie.

*****

The light from beneath the door dimmed to nothing as night fell. Nobody came to their prison nor were any external sounds audible. Time dragged and a new very faint light under the door suggested a rising moon. Both women were lying on the floor, their hands crossed under their heads, when a slight sound was heard. The door was slowly and silently opening. Angled moon rays penetrated the gloom and a small human figure stood silhouetted in the doorway. The familiar voice spoke in subdued tones.
"It is really Lucky. I've come to take you away from this dreadful place."
Both Connie and Bonnie gaped but it was the former who exclaimed "how the hell did you get here?"

"I was bad and did not listen to you. I hid under the old sacks in the back of the Land Rover. I was very quiet and you did not know was there. I wanted to come for the ride." he whispered.
"Lucky you're our lucky mascot!" how did you know what had happened to us and where we were?" Asked Bonnie.
"I looked out from under the sacks and saw what happened after you had tea with that terrible fat man and the other two. I stayed where I was until it was dark and then crept round the back of the house. I saw this building with a big wooden bar across the door and was hoping you are here and you were. I'm so happy but I'm also bit frightened." explained the boy.
"Lucky you earned yourself one hell of a bonus if we get out of here alive. Did you see any guards or dogs around the house?" queried Bonnie.
"No, there are no dogs near here but only many down near the gate. Also, I hear dogs barking near the fence." replied lucky.
"Where is the Land Rover now and are the keys still in it?" asked Connie.
In whispers the three discussed the situation and then moved. They crept out of the building one by one and Bonnie, the last to leave, closed the door and replaced the bar. In single file and keeping close to the wall they circled the courtyard to an open archway which led to a vegetable garden. They slowly made their way between the vegetable beds, guided by the light of a quarter moon, until they found themselves in uncultivated ground covered in long grass and strewn with granite boulders of all sizes.

Carefully they followed the contour, skirting the large boulders, round to the front of the house. The Land Rover stood silent where they had left it. When they reached it, Bonnie checked that the keys were in the ignition and then released the handbrake. All three pushed hard as they could until the vehicle moved gradually backwards. Bonnie turned the steering wheel and then they all pushed again. This time the Land Rover started to roll on its own down the hill. The three jumped in. Light showed from the window of the mansion but nobody seemed to have stirred.

With Bonnie at the wheel the Land Rover glided slowly down and around the kopje. Near the bottom she turned the ignition switch, put the vehicle in gear and let out the clutch. The engine sprang to life still without lights and without revving the engine, Bonnie drove slowly along the road between the ghostly silhouettes of the gum trees. About three hundred metres from the gate, she tramped the accelerator and switched on the headlights.

Ahead was a scene of pandemonium. At least a dozen guards in various stages of undress poured from the guard house trying to adjust their clothes and ready their weapons at the same time. The Land Rover swept towards the gate at high speed. As it was just about to connect with a steel mesh structure, two guards dived sideways to safety.

There was a terrible sound of rending metal and they were through. One half of the gate hung drunkenly on the left-hand fender for a few seconds before falling off sideways. Above the sound of the roaring engine, all three occupants of the racing vehicle heard the staccato stammer of several automatic weapons. Bullets buzzed above their heads.

Bonnie drove for at least ten minutes before she pulled the Land Rover to a halt to assess the damage. There was little and then only superficial; a few dents in the bodywork and a slightly bent front fender which had taken the brunt of the impact. Through the night they drove in silence as each calmed down and collected their thoughts.

The night porter gave the trio a most peculiar look as they filed through the hotel foyer at three in the morning. The girls insisted that Lucky accompany them. In the privacy of their room they each gave him a hug and a thick wad of notes. Lucky solemnly but firmly returned the money with the admonition, "no more money! I only do my job."
With this he curled up on the floor with a cushion beneath his head and promptly fell asleep. Within minutes Bonnie and Connie were in this same physical state.

*****

The day dawned humid and hot but unnoticed by the three whose night had been one to remember. They rose shortly before noon and shared an early lunch in the room. After lunch they drove to Sam Chiweshe. He surveyed the damaged Land Rover but lost none of his joviality. In fact, it increased at the site of the folding stuff that Connie proffered. He "repaired" the damage immediately with a couple of swings of a fourteen-pound hammer, oblivious of the flakes of paint that flew to the ground with each blow. He beamed as he surveyed his handiwork.

The scene in the "Kraal" had barely changed; the same tired band, the same overeager stripper and the same unsteady gait of Michael John Dunne as he walked onto the stage. Bonnie passed a waiter a banknote and a folded piece of paper. The money he placed in his pocket and the folded piece of paper he placed on the small table next to John Dunne's drink. At the end of his act the singer finished his drink and only then opened the note. He looked up in the direction of the two women. Stumbling slightly, he approached the table and with an exaggerated bow, introduced himself.
"Michael John Dunne. To what do I owe the pleasure?"
As he spoke he lowered himself into a vacant chair facing Bonnie and Connie.
"Captain Dunne, if you will listen to me for a few moments, you can then decide if it's a pleasure or not," said Connie.
She carried on, "I am Consuela Bojangles and this is Boncherie Armatrading. We have learnt a fair bit about you and wish to avail ourselves of your services."
Michael John laughed, "As a singer?"
"No, as a soldier." Connie replied.
Bonnie joined the conversation, "we need your help to recover

something that rightfully belongs to us or at least to our principles. We will have to take it by force and according to your CV this should be right up your street."

The smile faded from his face and he said quietly, "you've got the wrong man. I was a soldier but now I'm nothing more than an alcoholic singing fool."
Bonnie persisted, "you're the man we want. We'll give you time, a reasonable amount of time, to get that monkey off your back. In fact, we will help you all we can. In addition, we offer you four thousand dollars for the job we want doing, with a bonus at the satisfactory conclusion. How about it?"

Michael John looked at the speakers through bloodshot eyes. He said nothing as he conducted a mental debate of his own. There was a silence for nearly ten minutes, uninterrupted by the two women. At last he looked up and said, "for a long time I've hated myself for the way I live and make a living. If you believe in me to the extent of offering me a hand out of the gutter and the job to boot, I'm your man." A quizzical smile now crossed his face.
"Done!" cried Bonnie excitedly.
It was Connie who got down to specifics and said, "I suggest we take you away for a couple of weeks to dry out, forgive the expression. Where would you suggest?"
Michael John did not hesitate, "The Vumba." was all he said.
"Right, The Vumba it is, wherever or whatever it is," said Connie

The women left the nightclub to return to the hotel having agreed with Michael John that they would make an early start for the Vumba Mountains the following morning.
Michael John was to arrange hotel bookings and meet them at the Monomatapa. They would travel in the Land Rover.

Lucky was disappointed to hear the news that his services would not be required for a couple of weeks. He did not, however, have much trouble in understanding what was meant by retainer and pocketed it with some glee.

*****

Chapter 9

From Harare they traveled east towards Zimbabwe's border with Mozambique. They passed through a succession of small towns who obviously owed their existence to the surrounding maize and tobacco farms. Three hours after leaving Harare they reached the border town of Mutare which nestled in a hollow surrounded by substantial mountains.
Having filled their vehicle with petrol, they drove into the eastern mountains, The Vumba. Initially they drove along a tarred road but after about twelve miles the tar gave way to gravel.

A further ten or so miles along the gravel road ran along the substantial crest of a ridge then dropped fairly steeply to the east. At the next junction, the Land Rover turned right, following instructions on a rustic signboard. Now the road wound through a series of bends. Where the gravel had worn thin the rich soil beneath showed through as a rich red brown, a sign of the high fertility of this land which coupled with the high rainfall, supported the coffee crop for which the area was famous. The shadows of the trees dappled the road and hid many of the bumps and corrugations that rattled the vehicle. Many of the trees were original members of the indigenous forests that once carpeted the Vumba Mountains. They now fought for their existence against the insidious but persistent encroachment of the alien black wattle

The trees backed away from the road and revealed the turnoff to the hotel. Bonnie swung the Land Rover right into an avenue of massive gum trees that retained a regal look despite the strips of untidy bark that hung darkly on their pale green trunks. The gums gave way to rolling green lawns and a massive pond decorated with numerous water lilies. On the edge of the pond stood a derelict watermill and an abandoned belvedere.

For some time now, Michael John, though still sitting in the back with shoulders hunched forward, had picked his head up and was obviously conscious of the ever-changing scenery that passed them. His interest was that of an old lion who returns to the hunting area of his youth and savours the smells and sights which once stirred his killer instincts.

Beyond the pond the road forked to form a wide loop that gave two-way entry to the front of the hotel. The building looked, at first glance, misplaced. It revealed itself as a massive castle with towers and turrets that surprisingly lacked incongruity as it stood framed by the natural forest that threatened to overwhelm it from behind.

When the Land Rover came to a stop, Michael John made no move to leave the vehicle and follow the two girls who skipped up the steps to the reception area. He was overcome by another uncontrollable shaking fit. He stilled his trembling hands by pushing them, fists clenched, down into the pockets of his old camouflage jacket. A few minutes later the girls returned accompanied by a porter. Michael John insisted on carrying his own two cases more as a need to occupy his hands than to preserve any sense of manhood. The group trooped through the reception area and followed the porter up two flights of iron balustraded stairs. The first door the porter opened revealed a large circular room which occupied the entire area of one of the turrets. Casement windows opened out onto a view of the hotel's lawns and beyond that a series of mountains and valleys and finally, in the distance, gave way to the flat plains of Mozambique. The room, tastefully furnished in possibly genuine period pieces was dominated by a large, double four-poster bed. The porter opened the second door to indicate the interleading single bedroom.

Michael John's hand made a move towards his pocket but Connie beat him to it and handed a note to the grateful porter.
Bonnie surveyed the accommodation. "Nice, very nice. Where does darkest Africa come in?"
Michael John replied "it should be nice. The British Royal Family had

this suite for a week when they stayed here donkey years ago. Paying a pretty package aren't you?"
"Dear man, that's none of your business, but it is largely up to you to make what we are paying worthwhile, understood?"
"Okay, okay, I'll do what you want, that's what I'm being paid for!"
This caused an outburst from Bonnie, "listen friend, we need you and we're prepared to pay for it, but don't forget you need us if you want to be anything other than the bloody wreck you are now!"
Michael John stood admonished. He picked up his cases and went into the smaller room.
Outside the relative coolth of the stonewalls, the mountains shimmered in the heat haze. Insects buzzed and droned in the mid-afternoon sun but the heat and humidity had driven all other animals to shade in silence.

Connie stood at the into-leading door and looked at the man who sat dejectedly on the bed. His eyes look darker and more cadaverous. He had the shakes badly now. Connie turned away only to return a minute later with a valium which she pushed between his chattering teeth and followed it with a mouthful of water from the glass she held. She then led him like a little boy to the bathroom ensuite with the larger bedroom.
"Get in there, under a cold shower and try and relax." she said with authority. Michael John complied.
Twenty minutes later he emerged from the bathroom clad only in a towel, his prematurely grey hair wetly plastered to his head. His eyes registered shock at the two lying on the double bed clad only in the briefest of bikini pants. Two pairs of breasts stood proudly up from the reclining bodies, defying the laws of gravity.
Michael John gasped, "what the hell are you to up to? You're playing with me, teasing me. What in God's name do think you're doing?"

He received no verbal reply from either. Bonnie got up from the bed and went to Michael John who was by now making his way towards the

other room. She grasped his hand in hers and guided him to the brass four-poster. She eased him down so that he lay comfortably close to Connie. She gently turned him onto his front so that his hands lay by his side and his head sagged sideways on the pillow. Nimbly she swung herself over him to sit on the small of his back. Her breasts hung deliciously downwards as she leaned forward and expertly started to massage the muscles of his shoulders and neck. As her fingers plied the tense muscle fibres, she felt the tension of years of trying to fight fate slowly disappear. A smile crept across Michael John's rugged face and his eyes closed slowly. Minutes past and then he was asleep. Connie turned her head and lightly kissed him on the nose. She was aware of a smell of soap from his sun darkened skin and the now clean, healthy smell of his breath.
"He really is a bit of all right" she said as her gaze swept over his strong body only slightly thickened at the waist by years of wrong living.
"Yes, we'll soon have him firing on all cylinders and I mean all cylinders." said her blonde companion with a wink. Michael John slept and Bonnie and Connie took their time over showering, a manicure and make up. He awoke feeling more refreshed than he had for years. He lay back and gazed peacefully at the two, both dressed in skimpy halter neck dresses that barely attempted to disguise their figures. They sat in two easy chairs, smoke from Connie's cigarette drifting lazily upwards, its twists and spirals plainly visible as they drifted across the almost horizontal rays of the setting sun, beams of light that entered the west facing windows and played on the opposite wall of the room.

Michael John's shakes seem now little more than an easily concealed tremor of his hands. His mind was drifting easily on a shallow cloud of valium induced narcosis. However, in deference to his wish, Connie phoned the reception and arranged for room service to bring dinner later. Michael John felt better but not ready yet to guide food to his mouth with unsteady hands, subject to the gaze of the hotel's other guests.

To while away the time until dinner the three wandered out of the hotel and down the neatly mowed lawn to the pond. With the dying of the sun, both the excessive heat and humidity seem to lessen. Cicadas tuned their hind legs in preparation for their nightly concert and a nightjar awoke and started it's strident call. Bonnie and Connie sat quietly on a bench and breathed with pleasure the sweet scent that wafted towards them from the nearby mimosa tree. Michael John sat on a rock at the edge of the pond and picked up a succession of flat pebbles which he expertly skimmed across the pond surface, some to land on the other side, some to snag on the edge of water lily leaves to sink into the now dark water. There was no malice in the way he skimmed the stones and Connie and Bonnie knew that he was firmly planted on the road back.

The girls were more than a little surprised at the dinner that was wheeled into their room on a hot-tray shortly after eight. A passable consommé was followed by a more than passable crumbed trout stuffed with capers. Michael John explained that the trout were readily available, raised commercially, only a few kilometres away in ponds fed from cold mountain streams. The next course was a succulent tornado Rossini, neither raw nor cindered. Any gastric cavities were finally filled with a zabaglione that would have done credit to that master chef, Fellini of Vito's Tavern in Mayfair.

The only sound in the silent night was the occasional faraway bark of a farm dog. So ended the first day of Michael John's journey back to normality.

*****

The rays of the rising sun picked out the three figures in vests and running shorts that left the still silent hotel and pounded along the track across the golf course. The track passed through a gap in a grove of closely spaced old pine trees. Beyond in the shadow where the sun could not yet reach, the air was bracingly cool. Connie and Bonnie ran on easily but Michael John started to flag. His breath now came in rapid grasps, sign of thousands of harsh cigarettes and equally harsh double brandies. Nevertheless, he kept on. The girls adjusted their pace to his. They broke away from the track to run uphill along a deserted fairway. Their feet left wet footprints on the dew spattered turf.

Near the top of the hill they stopped at a fence that marked the boundary of the golf course. Across the fence not faraway stood an iron roofed stone dairy. Healthy black-and-white Friesian cows milled around outside awaiting their turn in the stalls. The scruffy figure in an old Army greatcoat moved towards the fence. He stopped across the wire from Michael John, his old face creased and smiled.
"Mangwanani, Dangarare!" He shouted gleefully.
Michael John replied in Shona with obviously equal pleasure. Bonnie and Connie stood by patiently but not a little surprised, excluded from the rapid and animated conversation that took place in the alien tongue. Eventually the two talkers completed their verbal interchange and broke off, the old African to return to his bovine charges and Michael John to grin sheepishly at his companions.
It was Connie who admonished him, not unexpectedly, as he was fast coming to the conclusion that she was the more shrewish of his two employers.
"He knows you." She accused and continuing "you didn't say anything yesterday about knowing this part of the world. Did you?"
Michael John looked down into liquid amber eyes shot with anger that transfixed him.
"You never asked me" came the quick retort "of course I know the area. I know it well. I spent the best part of two years based in Mutare during the war. I've covered just about every bush track and forest trail

between here and Inyanga chasing terrs, sorry, freedom fighters. We had a lot of contacts in this area too. Old Amos there" he pointed with his head at the old man coaxing a cow into the dairy by painfully twisting its tail, "he's an old friend, the old reprobate! He wisely sat on the fence for years. He impartially supplied information to both the security forces and the other side. Doesn't seem to have done him any harm. Still has the same job and probably the same dirty hut full of grovelling wives are snotty-nosed kids."
The anger faded from Connie's eyes as understanding came to her.
"Actually, that's super, Michael John. I think this is the most beautiful part of the world I have ever seen. We'll get you fit and well again and you can be our guide; show us all there is to see in the Vumba."
"A bargain! I'll show you every lovely bit of what I think is one of the last almost unspoiled parts of our country." replied Michael John with pride in his voice.

They retraced their steps to the hotel as the sun started to make its presence felt. Without prompting, Michael John joined Connie and Bonnie in the dining room and all three did justice to a real English breakfast. Michael John halted the piece of toast, liberally coated in genuine Roses lime marmalade, that was moving towards his mouth and offered, "I tell you what we'll do after breakfast. I'll take you to Manchester Gardens. You'll love it! And from there I'll take you down to Rusty Morgan's coffee farm next door."
"Marvellous" said Bonnie as she quickly drained her coffee.

The Land Rover wound its way back to the avenue of gum trees beneath the rocky overhang of "Chinakwaremba", Leopard Rock, after which the hotel took its name. Though it had rained only two days previously, twin trails of dust rose from the back wheels of the vehicle and chokingly engulfed the occupants each time the Land Rover slowed at a junction or a turn.

A few kilometres back along the road to Mutare, Michael John, now driving, swung off the main district road downhill to the gates of Manchester Gardens, now called the Vumba National Park. The ranger in attendance at the gate knew him and after a few cheerful words in Shona, waved them through without a charge. As they slowly drove through the gardens taking in one beautiful scene of horticultural perfection after the other, Michael John told the girls of the history of the place. Many years ago, when the beauty of the Vumba was as yet largely undiscovered, a man had come, named Taylor, he thought, who had made a fortune in cotton in his native Lancashire. He had ploughed a large portion of his wealth into what he called Manchester Gardens. Over the years his money tamed a large area of the wilderness and put in its place acres of lawns and pools and exotic flowers whose sheer abundance more than compensated for the loss of the virgin forest.

They had stopped and left the Land Rover to delight over the Egyptian Goose and the goslings who played amongst the hyacinths dotted over a small pool when an unpleasant incident took place. A small, rather swarthy man approached across the grass. He was dressed all in khaki with green socks and epaulettes that pronounced him to be the park warden.
"Ah come to gloat have we, Dunne? Come up in the world have we? And such lovely companions!" he smirked through fleshless lips.
Michael John, who had noted his approach in silence turned on him, a fist raised and snarled "bugger off you sodding little runt!"
Coombe, the runt of a ranger, did as he was told but threw over his shoulder as he took his departure, "still the great warrior, still the great Selous Scout, Dunne?"
Michael John felt an explanation was necessary, "he was my sergeant for a short while. He ran in terror from a contact and I had him bust to troopy and he's never forgiven me."
Connie and Bonnie accepted his explanation and soon forgot the incident.

*****

After a picnic lunch the hotel had provided, they moved on to Rusty Morgan's estate which nestled in the valley below the park. Rusty Morgan with his florid face, flaming red hair, deerstalker hat and walking stick would not have been out of place on an English country estate. The girls warmed to him as he did to them and he took an obvious pleasure and pride in showing them acres of orderly rows of coffee trees whose polished dark leaves scarcely concealed the luscious masses of ripening berries. In one plantation women and children quickly selected the darkest red berries and deftly nipped them off the branches and into sacks. He showed them the factory with its pulper and fermentation tanks and seemingly miles of hessian covered racks on which the already fermented coffee lay drying under an almost cloudless sky.

After numerous cups of homegrown, home roasted coffee, they took their leave of the jocular widower but not before Rusty had whispered into Michael John's ear "you lucky devil, you!" Michael John smiled in agreement but mentally noted that he was not quite sure as to the extent of his luck as pangs of thirst for alcohol were beginning to rack his insides and doubts about the so far, only briefly explained job he had to do, crept into his mind.

Michael John somewhat reluctantly joined Bonnie and Connie at dinner. The thunderstorm that brewed outside stirred up a restlessness in him that he found hard to conceal, more so as he forced himself to sip orange juice as the other two put away two bottles of Tasheimer with obvious pleasure. The dinner was as much a gastronomic experience as that of the night before, but it failed to soothe him. He refused to take coffee in the lounge with the other two after dinner and went straight to their suite.

When he came out of the bathroom having soaked in a tepid bath for over half an hour he found Connie and Bonnie already in the double bed in the room lit only by a bedside lamp of rather limited wattage. Michael John moved towards the other room to sleep in solitude as he had wearily done the night before when a movement caught his eye. Bonnie crooked her index finger at him. As if mesmerised he obeyed the summons and climbed under the bed clothes between the two exquisite naked female forms.

Years rolled away from him as first one then the other of the nubile temptresses teased his earlobes with wicked little teeth and kissed him on the lips and neck and chest, while all the time probing hands skimmed over his skin and pressed and stroked his body. Time after time he took one and then the other and gave himself completely to the exquisite tension and then release that came with each climax. At last he could respond no more and fell immediately into deep sleep, his head cradled against Bonnie's breasts and his back warmly fitted into the crook of Connie's body behind him.
Bonnie whispered through the strands of Michael Johns hair,
"This beautiful beast is not quite the wreck we thought he was, is he Connie?"
A contented sigh of affirmation came muffled from behind Michael John.

*****

The days that followed were largely distinguishable by the visits to places of interest that the trio made in between strenuous runs, long sets of tennis and including swims in the large swimming pool where they were normally to be found at the hottest part of the day. Michael John's body healed. His waist thinned, his eyes cleared and a deeper, healthier tan glowed on his skin. His mind too, was healing as his longings for a drink became more and more spaced out and he could now watch his companions sip ice-cold lager at the poolside without regret. More and more he was conscious of a deep feeling of gratitude to the two whose bed he happily and energetically continued to share. He felt not only gratitude but now a feeling of love and protectiveness towards them which aroused in him a determination to make what he had soon to do for them a success.

Chapter 10

It was late one night well into the second week of their stay in the mountains. The three of them lay naked on the bed. Outside it was pouring with rain, but inside the room the tepid air was still. They lay contentedly, conversation coming in fits and starts and centred largely on plans to deal with Courtney. Michael John smoked a cigarette, intermittently flicking the ash off into an ashtray perched on his bare stomach. Every time he did this the glow of the cigarette eliminated the still somewhat distended instrument of their mutual contentment.
"I'm ready now." he declared, stubbing the cigarette out.
"Are you sure? We still have a few days to go on our booking" murmured a sleepy Bonnie.
"Yes, and I'll prove it to you tomorrow!" Michael John stretched and continued, "I'm going to join the Royal Order of Chimney Sweeps."
"Oh yes, and we'll be the water babies and Kingsley himself will attend the investiture!" scoffed an also sleepy Connie.
"No seriously. There's a rock chimney on the face of Leopard Rock. It's one hell of a climb and if you make it the owners of the hotel give you a grand certificate and put your name in gold on the board in the pub. I reckon if I can make it that will prove to you that I'm ready for Courtney and any freaking army he can muster." Michael John said this with an authority in his voice that was not present ten days ago. Since no comment came from his two now half asleep companions, he turned over and closed his eyes.

*****

The owner of the hotel, Charles, stood with a small group of interested hotel guests in the deep shadows of the forest at the base of the cliff. "I'll see you started and then meet you at the top, if you make it." he offered disparagingly.

"I'll make it all right!" Michael John flung at him from his uncomfortable perch about ten metres up the vertical rock channel that was the chimney. He was wedged with his back against one rock face and his feet and hands pressing against the opposite wall. Pushing hard with his bare feet and clinging to any unevenness with this hands, he edged his back upwards a half metre. Then, back tight against the rock, he moved first one foot and then the other upwards; whilst his hands sought for any small rock outcrop that offered a handhold. He repeated the procedure over and over again and slowly moved up the chimney.

The rock faces were wet from the rain of the night before but this was partially compensated for by the roughness of the lichen that fought for its existence on the smooth granite surface. Sometimes a metre gain became a metre lost as friction failed, but slowly he clawed and eased his way towards the top. The rays of the morning sun did not penetrate the granite gulley but soon Michael John was drenched in sweat. Upwards he moved until about one hundred metres up he paused to catch his breath before attempting a particularly difficult section where the chimney widened considerably. The tendons of his legs and arms were taught as bow strings as he strove to maintain his difficult position. Having got his breath back a bit, he started to negotiate the treacherous section. From some twenty metres away a cruel voice mocked him.
"That's your lot. You won't make it. You're going to fall and break your bloody neck and I'm going to spit on your grave, you twisted cardboard hero!"
The voice came from Coombe, who Michael John realised had made an easy, shallow downhill approach from the top of the hill and was now positioned slightly around the corner from the cliff face on the grassy slope that characterised the less steep rear of the hill. Michael John said nothing as he started up again but more sweat broke out on his face and started to pour down his face. Doubts now assailed him. His concentration wavered. Both feet slipped and he fell. The fall was only the length of his body, his fingers extended rigidly at right angles to his hands, held to the slight horizontal flaw in the rock face. Pain wracked

his hands but he hung on. His toes found a rough patch and dug in. He now slowly arched his back into a position of relative security. Neither his body nor his mental reflexes had failed. Confidence flooded his mind and the rest was easy.

As he stood upright on the top of the hill both girls kissed him simultaneously. There was no sign of Coombe. Charles shook his hands with a bluff "Jolly good show, old chap. First new member of the order for years. Did it me'self in fifty four you know. Drinks are on the house tonight! "and he wandered off.

Michael John sat down to rest his tired body. He picked a piece of grass and chewed on the stem as he gazed out at the mountains before him, some at the same level as where he sat and others below that extended to the edge of the plains of Mozambique. The sunlight on the waters of Chicamba dam, a good thirty kilometres away, gave it a sheen of molten steel.
"I love these mountains" he said simply to the two women who sat beside him. "They accept me for what I am, let me wander over them in peace and want nothing in exchange. People aren't like that."
"Tell me more" encouraged Connie.
Michael John continued, "Try and understand. I was once a nobody, a tractor salesman, a real nobody and then the war came along. I found my niche in life. I grew up on a farm alongside the African. I learned their bush lore and their language and I used this as a soldier. I was a good soldier, not a smart saluting type soldier but a bush fighter and I found I loved it. I didn't particularly like the killing but it was just a part of it; a bit like hunting game as I did on the farm as a kid. And then they took it all away from me. The war stopped and I was a nobody again. That's why I drank, do you understand?"

The girls had listened in silence and realised they had just glimpsed behind the closed door of this unusual man's soul and they felt privileged. Connie hugged Michael John and her face close to his, was

conscious of the suppressed tears that welled up in his eyes.
"Michael John", she whispered, "you're a soldier again, our soldier and you're going to fight for us and for a lot of homeless kids in London."

Three figures, arms linked, walked off the hill, each lost in their own thoughts.

*****

On the morning of their last day in the Vumba, Michael John and the girls sat next to the swimming pool. Beads of moisture formed on the glasses of ice cold guava juice which they sipped from time to time. Michael John had surprised Bonnie and Connie with the cool calculating way in which he had put together a plan to overcome Courtney. In cognizance of his own abilities, it involved a direct and high-powered assault on Courtney's strongly defended empire. When it came to getting the necessary arms for the attack, Michael John produced the biggest surprise of all.
"No problem. I've already fixed it with Rusty Morgan."
"Rusty Morgan!" Bonnie and Connie gasped in unison, vision in mind of a figure more obviously suited to a role as a Father Christmas.
""I thought that would shatter you. Dusty was our quartermaster in the Scouts and a very good one. Near the end he cached away quite an arsenal. Said one day there would be a white coup in the country and arms would be needed. Hasn't happened yet but he's still hoping. He's giving us grenades, an RPG rocket launcher, some plastic explosive, couple of Uzis and plenty of ammo. Doesn't want a bean for it either. It's all good stuff. Okay?"
"That's marvelous" cried Bonnie, "you're an angel."
"An angel with arms and ammunition?" queried Michael John.
"I've got a bit of a treat for you tonight. I've arranged for you to meet Chioza. She's the local witch, well not really a witch, more like a spirit

medium. It is quite an honour that she has agreed. Like it?" he asked.
This was too much for Connie, the scientist, "Pull the other! I know, a harridan with pendulous dugs which you can't distinguish from the monkey tails around her waist!"
Michael John looked crestfallen but recovered at the obvious enthusiasm shown by Bonnie.

There was enough moonlight to light their way down the path that led from the hotel to the small village of huts that nestled in a forest clearing about a kilometre away. The lack of street lights combined with the stark shadows cast by the huge trees along the path caused Bonnie and Connie to feel uneasy, not at all as they would have felt in a jungle of the other kind, a concrete one. Michael John led them directly to a hut that stood away from the rest at the edge of the clearing. A wisp of smoke that filtered up through the thatched roof was just visible in the half light. He knocked on the door of hand hewn planks. A female voice answered and the three of them bobbed their heads and passed through the low doorway.

In the middle of the floor of stamped earth, a small fire blazed merrily and revealed an old crone dressed not in monkey tails but a shapeless grey dress. She sat on some kind of animal skin and the flickering of the flames showed her to be an ancient crone if the depths of the fissures that crisscrossed her skin were any gauge. Through eyes that appeared to glow yellow in the subdued light, she weighed up her visitors and then spoke to Michael John in her own language. Her voice seemed younger than her body. Michael John translated for the other's benefit.
"She says to welcome you. She can see that you search for the truth. She will ask the spirit, Ndao, to speak to you through her lips."
The crone stopped speaking and Michael John sat down cross-legged on the floor across the fire from her. Bonnie and Connie followed suit. The girls were acutely aware of a pungent smell in the hut that Michael John knew to be only the wood smoke blending with the smell of the tar that coated the roof and inner walls of the hut.

Chioza dug into a small hide bag that lay next to where she sat and from it removed what looked like pieces of orange bark. She dropped them into the fire. Clouds of pale yellow smoke billowed from the fire and engulfed the occupants of the hut. The smell to start with was slightly sickly but after a while it seemed to develop a more pleasant character. The three Europeans sat and stared at the old hag. As they watched, her body disappeared and her head seemed to hang disembodied in midair. They began to feel slightly drowsy but couldn't prevent themselves from staring at the head opposite, who's eyes pierced right through them. The head's mouth opened and a male voice started to speak. Michael John translated in a subdued whisper.
"I see you. You have come a long way from across the big water. You come as warriors. I see a giant and a dwarf that cross your paths. You win a great battle but I see a long journey that has as many twists and turns as the movement of a mamba. You will go now, but with my blessing."

The voice stopped. The body of the woman seemed to reappear and she sat rocking from side to side and quietly wailing in her own voice.
"It's over now" said Michael John and led the others out of the hut into the cool night air which soon cleared their minds. Bonnie and Connie felt shivers run down their spines at the thought of what they just heard.
"It was horrible but fascinating" said Bonnie much affected by the session, "the big water must be the sea, the giant must be Courtney and I suppose the dwarf could be Lucky but the long journey, I just don't know."

Chapter 11

The difference between the journey to the Vumba and the return journey which they now made back to Harare, was that now Michael John drove. The change wrought in the man in two weeks was almost unbelievable.

Standing on the steps of the hotel was a familiar figure who started jumping up and down, as soon as he saw the familiar vehicle. As they parked Bonnie remarked,
"Oh, poor little devil! He didn't know when exactly we were returning must have spent hours, even days waiting for us."
"Not a chance" interjected Michael John, "there's a thing called "bush telegraph" which we whites can never hope to understand. He would have been informed somehow, the time we would return, almost to the minute."
Lucky rushed up to the Land Rover and jabbered excitingly.
"Welcome back! Misses and Captain Dunne! There is a telegram waiting inside for you."
"Hi, Shorty." said both the girls as they climbed out of the vehicle. As they walked into the hotel Michael John explained that he had known Lucky for years and had often slipped him the odd dollar.

The receptionist greeted the party warmly and fetched two envelopes, one white and one orange, from the rack behind him. It was with some trepidation that Connie tore the orange telegram envelope open and her heart gave a great jump when she saw that the place of origin was Pretoria. The content was intentionally cryptic but to the point. "Regret bird flew cage stop red wheels smashed stop both bird and wheels died stop letter following stop Jannie".

Connie had read the telegram aloud to the others and their shocked reaction matched hers. Without a word she opened the second envelope. She read quickly and then enlightened her companions. In short, Jannie explained that for two weeks everything had gone well. He had kept Van der Westhuizen in the shed but had let him out for an hour a day to bath and exercise. The rest of the time he spent panel beating the Lotus until it was like new again and preparing meals for himself and Van der Westhuizen. Apologising profusely, he went on to admit that Van der Westhuizen was so docile that he had dropped his guard. The morning of the day on which he wrote the letter, he had taken Van der Westhuizen his breakfast. As usual he had unlocked the door and placed the tray on the floor in the doorway for Van der Westhuizen to pick up. As he was bending with the tray Van der Westhuizen had rushed him and as far as he could ascertain, hit him in the nape of his exposed neck.

When he came to, the Lotus had gone and Van der Westhuizen with it. He immediately jumped into his Daihatsu and without any definite plan in mind, set off along the road towards Pretoria. The ambulance and the police cars within a couple of kilometres of Geluk told the whole story. Van der Westhuizen had obviously taken a sharp bend at excessive speed, rolled off the road and hit a tree. Van der Westhuizen was dead. Jannie pulled up and decided to tell the police that Van der Westhuizen was a friend who had borrowed the car, the owners of said vehicle being away for a few weeks and the car had been left in his care. The police accepted the story had made no further enquiries.

Jannie ended the rather pathetic letter with a lot of self-recriminations and many apologies. As a post script he added that the Lotus was a write-off and hoped and prayed that it was insured.

Bonnie had listened in silence and when Connie had finished said, "Well that settles what to do with Van der Westhuizen. In a funny way I'm glad. It seems right for Manny...... an eye for an eye and a tooth for a tooth."
"I feel sorry for Jannie" said Connie, "that letter and telegram were posted four days ago. The poor devil has probably been stewing waiting to hear from us and especially to hear whether the Lotus is insured. I

think a prompt telegram is in order, don't you?"

From the room, a phonogram was despatched immediately which was to relieve Jannie of his anxiety vis-a-vis the insurance and to assure him that what had happened was probably for the best.

It was Michael John who suggested that there was no time like the present to hold a council of war to decide a strategy for the taking of Courtney and the Duiker Mine. He added that though the girls had filled him in as best they could as regards the situation at the mine and the surrounding countryside, proper plans could not be made without ordnance survey maps of the area.
Lucky who had been listening to what had been said immediately volunteered to run across the street to the government office which sold the maps.

Pending Lucky's return, the other three sat back and discussed "Operation Duiker" in general terms. Bonnie and Connie both emphasized that the object of the exercise was not so much Courtney, but his wealth. They knew that his house contained a fortune in antiques and works of art but, currency and emeralds were more usually negotiable and therefore of more use in redeeming the mortgage on St Mark's. As a last resort they would take the paintings and Persian rugs and smuggle them out of the country to London where with such acquaintances as the girls had, their conversion into hard cash at an acceptable discount would not be difficult.

The main obstacle to any plan was the presence of guards at the gate and on the perimeter fence of the property. Also, Adonis and Narcissus were always in close proximity to Courtney and his wealth.

Lucky returned with one map, in the centre of which lay Courtney's property, well demarcated. The twenty thousand acres formed a rough rectangle with the longer sides running approximately north to south.

Circles of close contour line showed that within the property these were in fact hills, the one on which the house stood and another which the girls and Lucky had not noticed simply because it was behind the house and was not visible from the entrance gate in the southern fence. They surmised that as they had circled up the hill towards the house, it had been hidden from view by the trees that flanked the road.

Michael John studied the map for some time in silence before he spoke. When he did he suggested without hesitation: "Right, this is the way I see it. We make our way in the Land Rover to a position not too far from the fence on the northern boundary of the property, preferably slowly so as not to create a tell-tale trail of dust and starting before dusk. Here we split. I will make my way round to the gate in the South. This will take me about three hours. I'll take the RPG and some grenades. In meanwhile you two……."
"hey what about me?" Lucky interjected.
Michael John continued, "you three will move quickly on foot to the fence, lay some plastic explosive charges, I'll show you how later, then I'll let fly at the gate and the gatehouse with the rockets. This will draw the guards to the gate. When you hear the rocket fire from the gate, blow the fence and go straight to the house in the Land Rover. With the two Uzi's you should be able to take out the two blacks and Courtney if necessary. I'll join you after having neutralized the guards and we help ourselves to what we want. How's that?"
"Marvellous, General Dunne! Said Bonnie "you lead and we'll follow!"
"I like it " added Lucky, scarcely able to contain his excitement.

Another day was drawing to a close and Michael John was anxious to return to his little cottage at Umwinsidale to check if his neighbours had fed his cat as promised. They therefore closed the planning session for the moment with the arrangement that everybody would rest up the following day and then meet for supper that evening at Michael John's place to make the final plans for the operations of the following day. Michael John took with him a suitcase they had purchased on the way through Mutare which contained the small arms, grenades and explosives. They decided to leave the RPG where it was, strapped to the underside of the chassis of the Land Rover, well out of sight.

*****

An early night was followed by a late rising. During the day the girls only left the hotel to purchase black denim jeans and hockey boots. Time passed swiftly as Connie taught Lucky how to play poker and Bonnie read a pile of magazines lifted from the residents lounge.

The drive to Michael John's cottage took the best part of half an hour. The road meandered at first through expensive suburbs and then through an attractive area bespattered with the characteristic msasa trees. Lucky sat in the back of the Land Rover and proudly gave name to every road and feature on the way. The approach to the cottage was over a small dam wall and then up to the top of the hill on which stood one of the smallest but also most attractive stone cottages that the girls had ever seen.

Nestling peacefully as it did, amongst tall trees, masses of flowers and exotic shrubs, it seem to reflect a side of Michael John's character that the girls did not realise existed. Michael John and cat greeted visitors and welcomed them to his untidy but quaint abode where they drank schooners of cold lager and ate vast quantities of curry. After supper they sat in the garden in the welcome cool of the evening and checked that everything was ready for the next morning. Lucky's contribution to the conversation was meager as he soon fell asleep on the grass next to the cat.

Chapter 12

Tensions suppressed conversation as the Land Rover retraced the route it had covered some two weeks before. The early afternoon sun beat down on the occupants of the open vehicle. By the time they had reached Gweru, all four were parched and extremely grateful for the cokes they gulped down at a garage, lukewarm though they were. With little time to go until sunset, Michael John guided the Land Rover towards Sherugwe.

From Sherugwe, he followed the road to the Duiker Mine until the girls judged that they were within about two kilometres of the gate. Without a second thought Michael John swung the Land Rover off the road to follow an erratic course dodging trees and anthills in a more or less north-east direction.

For twenty minutes or so he navigated by the position of the setting sun and with the last rays of the now fast disappearing red orb, they saw, not more than a couple of kilometres away, twin hills. Roughly in line with the two hills, the Land Rover came to halt. By instinct Michael John had pulled up the vehicle under the spreading branches of a flat topped tree, instinct demanding cover from the air.

From where they were they could see neither the fence nor the second hill on which the house stood, obscured as it was by the nearer hill. Michael John ducked under the Land Rover and quickly removed the RPG from its hiding place. He leaned over into the back of the vehicle and placed a number of grenades in an old Army rucksack and four missiles for the RPG. His own preparations made, he returned to the others.

"I make it six fifteen. I'm off and I should be in the vicinity of the gate shortly before nine. At nine on the dot, I will take out the gatehouse. When you hear the first explosion start the Land Rover and make for the

fence and lay charges as I showed you yesterday. Keep well back! A fair size piece of the wire mesh will disintegrate. The flash of the explosion won't be seen from the house and I'm sure that the bangs will be nothing compared to the ones I'll be making in the South."
He paused then continued, "Drive through the gap in the fence as fast as you can without lights. Skirt the first hill........ Oh! and I want Lucky to get off there and set up an OP on the hill. Then......."
Lucky started to interrupt but Michael John cut him short, "Lucky you're not armed and so that is the most useful job you can do for us! As I was saying, aim to hit the road from the gate just below the next hill and get up the hill as fast as you can. You might as well use the headlights from that stage on. Stop at the front of the house and empty a magazine each into the front door and all the windows you can see. Then get into the house and......."
"No need to say any more. We'll make a good job of it" said Connie confidently.

Michael John put on the rucksack, shouldered the RPG and he set off, throwing it over his shoulder, "Good luck! See you on the summit." The two women and the youth watched the figure clad in suede ankle boots, jeans and camouflage jacket fade into the gloom.

For the inactive three, time passed slowly. They sat in the Land Rover and listened to the sounds of the night, the mournful cries of the nightjar, the whining and buzzing of a million insects and the occasional distant bark of a dog. The moon rose and fought a to-and-fro battle with the clouds to illuminate the earth below. Occasionally one of the trio got out to stretch their legs and now and then a muted pop indicated a cool drink can being opened.

Time passed more quickly for Michael John as he silently padded southwards at a slight angle to where he imagined the fence to be. He had breasted the second hill and covered over five kilometres before he saw the silhouettes of the fence poles that stood sentry like in the dark.

He veered slightly away and carried on towards the target. Sometimes unseen branches brushed and scratched his face as he passed under the trees that frequently loomed into sight. Though the night was cool, Michael John was soon sweating beneath the heavy twill army jacket he wore, weighed down as he was by the arms he carried.

The luminous numbers on the dial of his watch showed the time to be just after half past eight. Michael John could plainly make out the guardhouse about fifty metres away and the fencing between it and him. He stepped behind a large tree. He swung his rucksack off his back onto the ground and removed three anti-tank missiles. One he loaded into the RPG launcher and the other two he placed nose down into each of the two large outer pockets of his camouflage jacket. The two grenades taken from the rucksack, were dropped gently into the spacious map pocket which he had once long ago sewn onto the front of the right leg of his jeans.

From the shelter of the tree Michael John crept slowly and quietly towards the gate. From the gatehouse came raucous and seemingly drunken laughter from some three or four persons. At the gate itself a lone figure stood with an AK automatic rifle butt down, held casually by the muzzle. His back was to Michael John. Ten metres from the gate, Michael John stopped and raised the RPG so it rested on his right shoulder. It was too dark to see the sights but his eyes could trace the line of the metal tube and he pointed it at the centre of the gate and fired.

First came the familiar whoosh followed immediately by the deafening explosion and blinding red flash. As the sound faded as suddenly as it had started, the centre of the gate was conspicuous by its absence as was the previously attendant guard.

A clamour came from the gatehouse as three disheveled guards burst through the door. Michael John had again readied the RPG. Without bothering to take accurate aim he fired a second missile in the vicinity of the door. Again, the tremendous explosion and a gaping hole in the wall. Two guards lay face down in the dirt. The third carried on running, accelerated by the blast towards Michael John whom he seemed not to notice as he passed through the non-existent gate and disappeared at a remarkable speed into the night. Michael John stood in the slight shadow of the damaged building and waited patiently. His patience was rewarded as a close group of four guards came running along the inside of the fence, AK's at the ready. A grenade rolled along the ground towards them and in a split-second four more guards were out of action. Then Michael John heard the sound of a heavy vehicle coming from the direction of the barracks. He ran along the road for a distance of about three hundred metres and dashed behind a tree at the side of the road. A matter of seconds later a seven ton lorry roared by. As it flashed past the uniformed men who packed the back were vaguely discernible. Michael John stepped out into the road leveling his RPG. As he did so it flashed through his mind that he was doing what the terrorists had often done to innocent travellers in the years of the bush war. Again, the whoosh as the missile sped into the back of the vehicle. The truck thundered, burning out of control into a large tree and its petrol tank exploded.

As silence descended once more, Michael John pictured in his mind the motorcycle he had seen parked at the side of the gatehouse. He ran easily back down the road and through the opening in the fence. From beneath a tree he retrieved the rucksack. Back in the gatehouse he gave a sigh of relief at finding the key in the motorcycle's ignition. He swung himself onto the saddle, leant downwards to switch on the petrol tap and then kicked. The machine started immediately. Guessing the gear positions, he pushed the gear pedal downwards and let out the clutch. The trees that flanked the road acted as a guide as he roared towards the kopje and Courtney's mansion. The cottages beside the road showed no sign of life. He slowed at the barrack building but again there was no sign of life. It appeared that he had neutralized most, if not all of Courtney's private army.

*****

The hollow boom of the first explosion reached the party at the Land Rover.
"That's it!" Cried Bonnie, starting the motor of the Land Rover. Travelling slowly, they approached the fence and stopped within twenty metres of it. Connie jumped out and ran forward with a cloth-enclosed bundle dangling from one hand. At the fence she placed the bundle on the ground and from it she took the plastic explosive which she moulded into a number of balls roughly the size of an egg. She pressed these into the wire mesh at metre intervals, up the fence then along the top for a couple of metres and then down to the ground again. Into each ball she pushed a pencil detonator with a short length of slow fuse. Using a lighter, she quickly lit the fuses and ran back to the others.
She had barely climbed into the Land Rover when a series of regular, almost genteel explosions fired. Several running metres of the fence had gone.

The going was rough and the Land Rover slewed from side to side hitting rocks and saplings. Luckily nothing of a more immovable nature barred their way. Bonnie guided the vehicle towards and then around the first hill. Halfway round they dropped a protesting Lucky to scamper to the top and stay there until called for. It was a forlorn figure who watched his friends drive off.

The sound of more explosions came drifting on the night air as Connie and Bonnie drew near to the base of the hill on the summit of which stood Courtney's mansion. Gingerly Bonnie eased the Land Rover across the ditch and onto the road at a point where it had just started to climb the hill. The Land Rover ascended. Before reaching the top, Bonnie brought it to a halt. The two women collected Uzis from the back and each pushed home a magazine and cocked the weapons. Another magazine each went into their pockets.

Stealthily they crept forward, their dark clad bodies invisible against the numerous shrubs that dotted the terrace in front of the house. They both stepped out from behind an oleander and then stood feet apart facing the front façade of the house. Not a light showed anywhere.

"Now!" Shouted Bonnie and double fusillades of nine millimeter parabellum bullets sprayed every window and the massive front door. In the silence that followed, each of the girls exchange magazines. Still the silence persisted and so with feelings of perplexity they advanced on the door, weapons at the ready on their hips. They paused, one each side of the door. Connie put her hand to the handle and slowly levered down, pushing at the same time. The door swung silently inwards, both Connie and Bonnie rushed into the entrance hall, first pressure on triggers already taken up.

Slanting moonbeams angling down through the open door, revealed a totally unexpected scene. The walls and floor of the hall were bare, gone were the valuable paintings and Persian rugs. They rushed from the hall into the lounge to be greeted by a similar scene. The ugly truth dawned on them. Courtney had skipped and taken everything of value.

The drone of a motorcycle engine grew louder and then died seconds later, Michael John burst into the house.
"Too late! The slimy sod has ducked!" cried Bonnie close to tears.
"Oh, sod it ! eliminated a whole bunch of guards, for what?" exclaimed Michael John.
Connie took a more rational view and said, "no use cursing and moping. Let's find out when he left, where he went to and get after him again."
"You're right. He's probably still in the country. You can't just walk up to a customs officer and say "one lorry load of valuables!" agreed Bonnie.
"You said that when you last came, the houses just off the road before you reached the barracks, were obviously inhabited. Perhaps they still are; probably by Courtney's mineworkers. We'll speak to them and hopefully they can give us a clue as to Fatso's whereabouts." suggested

Michael John.

The Land Rover's headlights illuminated a milling throng of men, women and children on the road. A grey-haired man in an old army overcoat approached the Land Rover and spoke Shona. Michael did his best to interpret as the ancient rambled on. "He says that we are miracle workers. He and his group are Courtney's labourers. They have been kept here under conditions of virtual slavery for over two years; no wages, poor food and never allowed off the property; the guards saw to that. They will do anything to help us now that they see they are free to return to their homes."
"What about Courtney?" asked an impatient Connie.
Michael John continue translating. "Only yesterday, a large truck arrived and went up to the house. It left about six hours later with Courtney and the "Devils Twins" as they refer to Adonis and Narcissus."

The old man and the other workers and their families were clapping and shouting as they crowded round their rescuers.
"The old boy also told me that behind the barracks is a large store of food, clothing and bedding. I think the best thing we can do is to open it and let these people help themselves while we get back to the house and see if Courtney's left any clues."

With this Michael John reversed the Land Rover back slowly along the road with the crowd in tow. He turned off at the barracks and taking one of the Uzis used half a magazine to shoot the lock to pieces on the store door. Men, women and children surged in, shrieking and laughing with the delight at the sight of such bounty. Back at the house Michael John switched on the lights and the three started to search. It was Connie who remembered Lucky and who left the other two to go and collect him.
Nothing of any value that was easily portable remained. Personal papers too, seemed to have been removed in their entirety. Heavy furniture, even some pieces of considerable value had been left behind. The opulence of the silk draped four-poster bed in the largest bedroom

upstairs, reminded them of Courtney and drove them on, tired as they were, in their search.

An interesting find, but of no importance was an outhouse which was the laboratory come factory, for the synthetic emeralds and emeralds there were, by the kilogram; trays of them stood on shelves casting an eerie, beautiful green glow on the walls. They examined a few of the larger stones and they were all flawless, a rare case where perfection came cheaper than imperfection. They left the stones where they lay.

Dawn was breaking as they eventually came to the sorry conclusion that Courtney had not left a single clue. Connie and Bonnie went into the kitchen and cooked a large breakfast from provisions Courtney had left behind. The breakfast helped not one iota in dispelling the feeling of failure that all four felt. They finished the food and prepared to leave. Walking through the entrance hall was Lucky who picked up the small pad next to the telephone and made to pocket it. Michael John saw the movement out of the corner of his eye.
"Hold it! Let me have a look at that." he said.
Lucky handed it over sheepishly, "I did not think you would mind me taking such a small thing." He tried to explain.
Michael John laughed, that's not why I wanted it. You can take whatever you like from this house. I just wanted to see if anything is written on the pad."

He examined the pad but all its pages were blank. He held the top page up an angle to the light. Impressions were visible. Taking the pencil from beside the phone, he gently shaded the page, and words sprang into view.
"P. O. Prepare Lord Lonsdale. Leaving soon. H de VC"
The other three leaned over Michael John's shoulders and also read what he had brought to light. They pondered about the words sometime before Bonnie offered:
"It looks like the text of a telegram he read over the phone, hence the PO

for post office. Presumably there is a friend of his, Lord Lonsdale. Must be an English peer. Looks like he's heading to England but how, with all he has to smuggle out of this country?"
"Well we won't get any answers here, stuck out in the bush. Let's get back to Harare and make enquiries." Connie suggested.

The whole property was deserted as they set off back to the metropolis. The workers and their families had gone. Silent reminders of what had happened on the night before were the burnt out truck at the side of the road surrounded by several mangled bodies and further corpses near the entrance, which seemed to have turned black. At close range they saw that the black was millions of voracious flies. They were all intensely grateful to leave the Duiker Mine and it's horrors behind.

Chapter 13

Bonnie lay on the bed alongside Michael John and played her fingers through the steel grey hair.
"You've been fantastic to us you know. It's not your fault that we have failed so far and we still have got more than enough money to pay you what we agreed."
"I don't need the money really and in fact I should be paying you for the way you have changed me." he replied, "I can't help feeling that Courtney is still accessible if only we can find him."

The bed they lay on and on which they had just made love, was Michael John's. It was at his insistence that they had checked out of the expensive hotel and installed themselves in his cottage at Umwinsidale. Even Lucky had joined them, insisting that since he was on their payroll, he should earn his keep. He pottered around the garden, plucked the occasional weed and watered the occasional flower. At night he curled up in the kitchen, oblivious of the discomfort of the hard quarry tile floor.

Connie walked into the bedroom, "I got through to Charlie Callan in London. Asked him for all he could get on Lord Lonsdale. He phoned back a few minutes ago. You two probably won't have heard the phone. Too busy I presume." She winked at the two on the bed and then continued, "it's rather puzzling what he has to say. Lord Lonsdale is four years old. He inherited from his father two years ago, his father having been killed in a car crash. His little Lordship lives with his mother in the manor at Kirby Lonsdale in Cheshire. Charlie couldn't help us anymore."
"Most peculiar. Perhaps we're barking up the wrong tree. Who or what else could Lord Lonsdale be?" said Bonnie from her horizontal position.

Michael John jumped up in all his nudity and explained "Who or what you said! I think I know what the answer is ! How about if Lord Lonsdale is either an aeroplane or a boat. I know that boats are usually given

female names but not always. Let's give it a try from this new angle."
"Agreed, but how would you start tracing an aeroplane or a boat, especially a boat since there is no shoreline in Zimbabwe?" asked Connie
"If it's a plane, I can get information from a friend in the Department of Civil Aviation. If it's a boat it's a problem. It could be almost anywhere on the Mozambique or South African coasts. That's one hell of a long shoreline. However, I think we can narrow it down a bit. I doubt the boat is in South Africa. If it was in South Africa, then Courtney could not be able to smuggle a truckload of goods through the South African customs; they're too strict. On the other hand, a couple of fat bribes would get anything through the Zimbabwe/ Mozambique border. So, if it's a boat, it must be moored somewhere on the Mozambique coast. I'll make some phone calls straightaway." replied Michael John at length.

He started to the bedroom door only to be stopped by Connie who reminded him of the state of undress. Unashamedly he quickly pulled on his underpants and shorts.

The call to the Department of Civil Aviation was short and sweet. Michael John's friend was a bit snooty. He stated that normal people did not name their planes, they referred to them by the registration letters. Michael John explained that the owner was not normal. He waited for a few minutes and got a firm reply: "Negative old chap".

Tracing a boat in another country was no mean task. Calls were made to the Commodores of every yacht club in the country. There was a blank every time. The Zimbabwean Ministry of Transport tried to help but had no registers of foreign vessels not even for Mozambique and so they drew another blank.

Michael John had run out of ideas, had settled into an easy chair and was sipping a cold beer when another possibility came to his mind. He remembered Eduardo Vaz, a transport contractor who ran a fleet of trucks up and down the length of Mozambique. He was one of the few

Portuguese who had stayed on after independence. He caught Eduardo taking a siesta at home in Beira. He answered the phone himself and it took some minutes of pleasantries before Michael John could get down to business. Eduardo did not recognise the name Lord Lonsdale but on being given a description of Courtney, hesitatingly suggested that he sounded like the owner of a motor yacht that he believed was moored at Tofo. Eduardo had an agent in Inhambane who he would contact after his siesta and report back to Michael John.

In true Portuguese fashion, it was not until hours later that the glad tidings came through from Eduardo. There was a vessel still moored at Tofo as of that morning and its name was Lord Lonsdale. Michael John could hardly contain his excitement as he listened to his Portuguese friend moaning about conditions in Mozambique and how many of his trucks the Renamo movement had destroyed on the Beira-Maputo run in recent weeks. At last Michael John managed to thank him and ring off. He dashed into the bedroom where Bonnie and Connie lay reading on the bed.
"We struck gold! The Lord Lonsdale is a fair sized boat moored at Tofo in Mozambique and was still there this morning. We'll get Courtney now, unless he's already on the way. I can check on that. I know the chap who owns the first garage you come to on entry into Mozambique. If Courtney's passed through he would have been sure to fill his truck there as the supplies further on are not very reliable." he said delightedly.

Without waiting for a reply, he dashed out of the room. Courtney could not have passed through the border apparently and a second call at six fifteen confirmed that he would not be doing so before the next morning as the border post had now closed. Michael John breathed a sigh of relief.
"Michael John you don't have to come with us you know." said Connie between mouthfuls of food.
"I know I don't have to but I'm coming with you. I wouldn't miss the showdown for anything." he replied, halting the mealie cob on the way

to his mouth. The mealie cob remained stationary has he carried on.
"I've been thinking. The border post opens again at six tomorrow morning. We'll leave here about three, drop Lucky in town and then head east. We should hit the border soon after it opens. Then we head for Tofo which I know slightly and wait for him there. Rather get him when he stops than try and stop him on the road. Okay?"
"Sounds fine to me, but aren't we cutting it a bit fine in our battered Land Rover?" asked Connie.
"We aren't going in the Land Rover. We're going in my Citroen. It's much faster and more comfortable and no arguments!" Michael John said firmly. Lucky pleaded to be allowed to come but this time the other three were resolute. He had no passport and that was that. They did concede however to his request that he be allowed to stay at the cottage until their return...

Chapter 14

In spite of the high daytime temperatures, there was a nip in the air at four o'clock in the morning, as the Citroen pulled out of Harare. The road was virtually deserted and very soon the car was speeding eastwards at a steady hundred and fifty kilometres an hour. Michael John drove. Bonnie sat beside him and Connie lounged on the backseat. The girls were surprised that the car, to them of vintage status, could eat up the kilometres with such smoothness and stability. Michael John explained that he had brought it new and in the intervening ten years had lavished much attention on it and at the same time rarely used it. With the hydraulic suspension set low it proved to be exceptionally stable at high speed.

The sun was just peeping over the horizon as they sped through Marondera, confident of the absence of any speed traps at this time of the morning. Incredibly, in some ten minutes less than two hours, they crested the ridge of the amphitheatre in the base of which sprawled a relatively small city they had passed through once before, Mutare. Here, Michael John pulled in at a petrol station and filled the Citroen up.
"Better have a full tank to start with. The supplies in Mozambique may be a bit chancy. I don't really know, not having been through for a couple of years." He explained.

Once over the ring of hills surrounding Mutare the still well maintained road wound down a series of slow curves to the border post. At the sight of the single-storey flat roofed building on the Zimbabwean side, memories flooded back to Michael John. A vision of himself dressed only in a pair of black running shorts and one hockey boot, crouched on the roof holding a 80 mm mortar with no baseplate but in its place the other hockey boot and pumping mortars at the customs and immigration building on the Mozambique side. He did this as fast as a grinning black sergeant could feed the bombs to him. He deftly dropped each one down the tube, ducked his head, waited for the whoof of the departing mortar shell, checked where previous mortars were landing and then corrected the angle of the tube before feeding in the next bomb. Could it be over ten years since that day when they plastered that building in retaliation for the 122 mm rockets that Frelimo had launched ineffectively from the Stalin organ parked safely in their own country; lobbing them over the hills into a defenseless and unsuspecting Mutare? He had not communicated his thoughts to the girls, afraid that they would not fully understand the exuberance he had felt that day... not just revenge but a genuine love of meaningful action.

Officials at the border posts only just open, were too bleary eyed to be friendly, officious or even efficient and so the formalities took up very little time. It was just after 6.30 as the car gathered speed along a reasonable tar road and continued east. Ahead lay still another eight hundred kilometres to Tofo, a distance which Michael John was confident could be covered in no more than six hours. In the unlikely event that Courtney was ahead of them, they would catch up with his truck somewhere on the last stretch along the coast between Vilancoulos and Inhambane.

The hum of the fast spinning tyres had an almost hypnotic effect on the occupants of the Citroen as it passed through country lower and flatter than that in Eastern Zimbabwe. The countryside itself seem to have a foreign character. The grass that grew right up to the tarmac verges was taller and the bush lusher and more dominant.

Intermittently, Michael John indicated places of interest, mostly related to his apparently rather frequent sorties into this part of the world as a member of Rhodesian security force groups involved in hot pursuit follow-up operations. Forty minutes from the border they could see in the distance the greasy surface of Chicamba Dam viewed from a much shallower angle than that from which they had seen it in the Vumba.

The first town of any size was Chimoio, which they bypassed without any slacking of speed. Beyond the Chimoio the country became more hilly and the road less straight. Michael John's driving gained the respect of Bonnie and Connie as he barely reduced speed. Open countryside gave way to patches or remnants of once magnificent indigenous tropical forest. At Gondola they managed to buy petrol and some cokes and wasting little time pressed on. Barely half an hour later they came to a T-junction at a cluster of buildings which bravely bore the name Inchope and Michael John turned right and south.

"The branch that goes straight on goes to Beira and the coast. The branch we are on is one of the last engineering efforts of the colonial Portuguese and runs all the way to Lourenco Marques, now called Maputo. We're going about halfway." Michael John explained.

Every kilometre or two there were large craters in the tar. They were not of recent origin and yet no attempt had been made to fill them in. Again, Michael John kept his foot down and the tyres of the Citroen complained every time they skirted a crater.
"Holy Mary! yelled Bonnie as she was flung violently against the car door, "is this meant to be a bloody obstacle course?"
Michael John laughed as he fought the steering wheel. "every time we dodge a crater, look off to the side of the road and you'll see the remains of a vehicle. These craters were caused by the landmines that Frelimo laid, perhaps as a going away present for the Portuguese and those rusty wrecks are the unfortunate cars and lorries that detonated the mines."
"Why the hell doesn't the government fill them in?" demanded Connie.
"Ah, well, there is a slight problem" replied Michael John.
"This part of the world is in the hands of Renamo, the resistance movement, who would only be only too pleased to fill them in with the bodies of anybody the government sent to fill in the craters!"
"Now he tells us" complained Bonnie, "what do we do if we meet up with this Renamo?"
"I don't know. Let's meet their problem when we come to it. We're better off than Courtney and his slow-moving lorry."

Kilometre succeeded kilometre as they drove south. They crossed a large river with the name Rio Save. Though the road was following the coast they saw nothing of the sea until they had bypassed Inhassoro and their first sight of the emerald green, olive, gold and purple mosaic of a true coral reef at close hand came with the entry into Vilancoulos where Michael John insisted on stopping for petrol. Bonnie and Connie, though hardly in a "enjoy the sights" frame of mind, were enchanted by their first sight of palm trees and coral strand. The sleazy hotel was still manned by a Portuguese gentleman who was obviously amazed at the arrival of the first foreigners he had seen for years. He rushed around waving his hands and shouting at an out of sight "Maria". Cold Laurentina beers and a Coke for Michael John soon graced the zinc topped table on the patio overlooking the sea. Saucers of bread cubes and small bowls of curried meat joined the drinks. The three tucked in and appetites whetted, agreed to Michael John's suggestion that they have a full meal. Michael John, surprisingly speaking fluent Portuguese, ordered a meal of prawns and calamari. He almost spoiled the pleasure of the arrival of the crustaceans and squid by disclosing that the delicious meat they had been picking at with tooth picks was in fact goat's meat.

*****

They all felt reluctant to leave the tropical paradise that was Vilancoulos but they still had quite a distance to cover before reaching Tofo. They continued down the coast through a land almost uninhabited. Only now and again did they see small clusters of huts crowding the road. Just over the crest of a small hill and with tall trees rushing past the car window, it happened. Not two hundred metres ahead of the speeding car, three figures in drab olive green uniforms stepped out of the trees and stood, legs astride, facing them. There was no mistaking the menace of the two AKs and RPG. that pointed at the car. Michael John hit the brakes and brought the Citroen to a halt about twenty metres from the three figures who maintained their stance in the middle of the road. Michael John opened his door and stepped out, his hands not actually raised but away from his body. One of the figures with an AK stepped forward and shouted at Michael John in Portuguese. His verbal delivery in a tone of anger and contempt continued for at least a minute. When they had finished, Michael John took over the speaking role, also managing a good minutes worth in a tone equally angry and contemptuous.

The girls meanwhile, had gingerly extricated themselves from the car and viewed events from the psychological safety of the open car door. Michael John turned around and in the tone of voice which communicated the gravity of the situation, explained: "They are Renamo as I suspected. They claim that this is their territory and don't take kindly to interlopers. They have generously declined to shoot us on the spot but insist on taking us, as prisoners, to their base camp not very far from here. They're their colonel, Fishaan, will decide what to do with us. We've got no option. We have to do what they want .....can't argue with AKs!"

"Oh lummy!" Bonnie moaned, "darkest Africa, Russian weapons, nobody knows who is running the country and that slob Courtney is going to get away!"

Directions issued in Portuguese and emphasized by pointing an AK were clear enough and Bonnie and Connie together with Michael John crammed themselves into the front seat of the Citroen while the three rebels did the same in the back. Following instructions, Michael John drove on down the Maputo Road for about three kilometres before turning right onto a barely visible overgrown track which traveled roughly west. The car bumped and swerved along the twin tracks for twenty minutes or so before it ran into a clearing of bare earth perhaps one hundred metres in diameter around the perimeter which stood a circle of thatch roofed huts. It stopped in front of the most imposing hut of the collection, more imposing only in the fact that it was the only one which had a veranda in front, the roof of which hung drunkenly down at one corner.

All the occupants of the car got out and moved towards the hut. Before they reached it the door opened and another uniformed figure stepped out. He looked absurd. He was only about one and a half metres high and almost as wide. He had a large head and the most outstanding feature of his face were the moist lips framing an immaculate set of white teeth. A peaked cap of the same material as his uniform balanced precariously on the top of his bald head.

The dwarf colonel and Michael John recognized each other simultaneously and rushed at each other. Connie and Bonnie immediately turned on the guards and were, in spite of the disadvantage of their unarmed condition, about to deliver deadly karate blows to the guards, when to their utter amazement, they saw that the two on a collision course were actually embracing each other.

Connie's anger at the sight of the two opposites, one tall and white, the other short and black, hugging each other affectionately was really only relief at seeing what she thought was a desperate situation instantly defused.
"Thundering boils! where hasn't Dale Carnegie reached? Win friends and influence rebels! What in God's name is on, Michael John?"
Michael John turned to face the girls, one arm still draped across the dwarf who fitted easily below his shoulder.
"You won't believe our luck! You won't believe this coincidence either. This is Cyprian, alias Fishaan and who I was thinking about only this morning. He used to be my mortar sergeant. By the way, Fishaan means short in their language; not inappropriate don't you think?"

Oblivious of the early afternoon sun that blazed down on them Michael John and Cyprian talked in the language unknown to the girls but by the

sound of it not Portuguese. Bonnie and Connie were starting to get restless when Cyprian barked some orders to his men who went into his hut and brought out four camp chairs and a folding table. He sat down and invited the others to join him. One of his men brought out of the hut a bottle of genuine whiskey, ice and some none too clean glasses which he placed roughly on the bare wooden tabletop. Cyprian half-filled each glass with the amber colored spirit and with his fingers put a lump of ice in each class. He pushed a glass in front of each of his guests and raising his own yelled, "Cheers! To yesterday, today and tomorrow!" The relevance of his toast escaped his companions but his over-cheerful manner and bloodshot eyes indicated that it was unlikely that it was the first of the day. They all raised a glass and Michael John apologised to the girls.
"I know I promised. No more booze but I daren't hurt his feelings. We need his cooperation and help."
"Okay," agreed Connie. "just this once." And drained her glass.

In deference to the girls, Cyprian continued to talk in English. Over three refills of their glasses, his story of how he came to be a colonel in the Renamo organization came out. As Michael John already knew, he was a member of the Matabele tribe and when independence came to Zimbabwe, he had been told by his superior officer, a Shona, that he would be no longer welcome in the Zimbabwean army. He had bitterly taken his leave and after drifting jobless for a year or so had heard that the Mozambican rebels were not fussy about the background of their recruits. His excellent training in the Selous Scouts and the warrior Matabele blood that ran in his veins more than compensated for his lack of height. In two years, he was a full colonel in charge of an area nearly the size of Ireland and had personally accounted for 47 government troops. He explained that the government only controlled the few towns in this part of the country. The countryside and its inhabitants were his.

Bonnie expressed the impatience of the others when she addressed Cyprian, "Col, all the time we are here downing whiskey with you, we're running the risk that the man who owes us a lot of money is going to get past us, get to Tofo and disappear over the horizon. We appreciate your hospitality but with your permission I assume we are free to go...... we'd like to press on."

Cyprian beamed at the speaker, "No panic, madams and Captain Dunne. I have the situation under control. The man you want has not passed through my area yet and in fact when he arrives my OPs will radio through immediately. They report every vehicle movement. I can assure you of at least two hours warning. I knew for example that your white Citroen was moving south at least two hours before you were brought here. So, let's fill our glasses and make a dead man of this bottle. Cheers!"

They resigned themselves to finishing the whiskey but, while they did so, sounded out Cyprian as to the location of Courtney's boat which was indeed off Tofo and had, what's more, been prepared to sail. Cyprian suggested they leave fairly soon, not before the departure of the last of the whiskey though, and make direct for a certain cottage on the hill overlooking Tofo and owned by a man sympathetic to the rebel cause. There was a radio there and Cyprian would be able to contact them to warn of Courtney's approach. The arrangement seemed ideal and was readily agreed to.

Chapter 15

The sun was dipping towards the purple hills far to the west and the whiskey bottle was dry. After much show of affection on all sides, they got into the Citroen and set off again. In the long shadows of the late afternoon, the track was hard to follow. At the main road Michael John swung the car right and soon they were speeding south again in fifth gear. Michael John slowed as they passed through a sleepy little town called Maxixe. Just outside of Maxixe, he took a left turning and the narrow tar road they traveled skirted a long narrow bay. The next town they reached was Inhambane which stood across the bay from Maxixe. Knowing Courtney was at least two hours behind, they took time to stop in Inhambane for petrol and a small supply of provisions. It was a pleasant little town with palm trees lining wide streets, pavement cafes and a small pier sticking out into the bay from which a ferry plied day and night to Maxixe, only a few kilometres across the water.

Michael John knew his way about this part of Mozambique and did not hesitate to take a rather badly kept tar road north east out of town over a sandy peninsula to the sea again. In the dwindling light, palm trees stood soldier-like in stepped ranks in plantation after plantation, through which the road wound. The road ran up a large sand dune and then down towards the sea. Before them lay a scene of incredible beauty. Tofo was a small cluster of houses which clung to the sloping side of a sand dune which overlooked a wide bay lined by a snow white beach and fringed by the inevitable palm trees.

Extending out to sea from the water's edge was a coral reef whose minimal depth below the sea made possible the site of the incredible patchwork of different colours now only visible as a series of shades of black and grey. In amongst the dark greys of the coral heads was a patch of white which indicated a break in the reef and a sandy bottom. In silhouette, against the lighter background were three craft, visibly bobbing gently at anchor. The offshore direction in which they swung at their moorings suggested an outgoing tide.

One of the three boats was much larger than the other two and fitted the description of Courtney's Lord Lonsdale. No lights showed on board but perhaps they were not yet warranted. The fall of night would prove more certainly whether there was anybody on board.

Enquiry at the small Miramar hotel elicited directions to Antonio Antunes's house, only a short distance away, halfway up the hill. Antonio proved to be a large coffee coloured man of mixed Portuguese and African parentage. He was expecting them and welcomed them to his humble house, rundown and dusty as it was. Scrawny chickens scratched around the yard and an equally scrawny wife scratched around the house. Antonio gave them a room for their use, temporary as their visit was to be and showed them the ablution facilities in the form of a long-drop toilet, a hand water pump and zinc tub in the garden. The three were tired and hungry and after washing some of the road dust off their hands and faces at the pump, were pleased to tuck into large bowls of boiled dried cod done in onion and tomatoes and accompanied by rice.
Bonnie and Connie took no part in the desultory conversation that took place at the dinner table because it was conducted in Portuguese. Anything of interest Michael John passed on to them. A stroke of luck came their way in the form of an inflatable dinghy which Antonio possessed. It had no motor but this was of no consequence for, if they were to take Courtney by surprise, they would have to approach his boat as silently as possible. Paddle power was the only answer.

The radio stood on the floor next to Michael John's chair. Michael John had made contact with Cyprian's callsign 'Charlie Tango' and received the news that there was no sign of Courtney as yet. Michael John sat up, stretched and moved to the edge of the veranda. He gazed down at the scattered lights of the houses below them and at the shimmering band of silver reflected off the sea by the rising moon. Such a scene of

tranquility seemed incongruous in this trouble torn country. He turned to address Connie and Bonnie who sat silently savoring the cooler air, an invigorating respite from the searing heat of the day.
"We don't know if he's going to arrive today. We can't just all sit up and wait. We'll all be buggered tomorrow. I suggest we set watches. You two can take it in turn from now, nine o'clock until 12 and then till three and I'll take the three to six watch. Okay?"
"Suits me," said Connie, "but I'm not sleeping in that filthy room Antonio has given us."
"Bring the mattress out here on the veranda and I'll get a rug from the car. We'll sleep under the stars. How's that?" said Michael John.
"Marvellous. I'll take the first watch and you two kip," answered Bonnie. Michael John and Connie curled up on the mattress with an old cushion under their heads and a rug over their bodies. Soon they slept while Bonnie sat with her feet on the table. Occasionally she smoked and when she did the lighted end of the cigarette glowed like a beacon in the semi-dark of the moonlit night. At midnight, she nudged Connie awake and took her place next to Michael John who stirred but didn't wake. Connie repeated the process at three with Michael John.

*****

Dawn revealed a cloudless sky and already the local inhabitants were about their business. Dark blobs on the water beyond the reef were the fishermen attempting to scrape a living from the sea. Women in colorful headscarves went to and fro between the more humble dwellings and the well. Twists of smoke indicated that the first meal of the day was on the go. Antonio's wife served breakfast on the veranda, succulent pawpaws, black coffee and buttterless chunks of bread. The somewhat refreshed and hungry trio tucked into the basic but adequate fare. Invigorated they might be but an element of concern tinged the conversation at the breakfast table.

"Not a light, not a sound, in fact not a bloody anything all night'." complained a clear eyed Bonnie.
"Michael John be honest with us. Do you think that we have misinterpreted the message on the pad and that slimy, sexually sick son of a bitch has left by plane or by some other means?"
"I'll stake my life he's coming here to Tofo. It's not just the message but also the fact that he can't just put his paintings and silverware and of course, all the money and emeralds onto a plane and take off. There's also the boat down there. She's worth a packet and he's not going to up and leave her. The easiest way for friend Courtney is to get the stuff through the Zimbabwean and most of beacon borders with the aid of hefty bribes; get it on board and make for some port in Europe. I feel sure about it" said a confident Michael John.
He continued, "I spent days in OP's ambushes wondering if it's all a wild goose chase but, if your information is correct, something always happens in the end. In the meanwhile, we're sitting in one of the most beautiful places on the African coast with a reliable warning system. We've just got to be patient and wait." The girls seemed somewhat mollified and in consequence started to be more aware of their surroundings.
"Sea looks grand to me. Wish we could have a swim," ventured Connie .
"No problem," offered Michael John. He got up and went into the house and the girls could hear him talking to Antonio's wife. When he returned he told them, "I've fixed for Antonio's wife to keep a listening watch on the radio and if anything comes through for us, she'll stand on the veranda and waive a towel or something as a signal. So, let's go!"
'There's another problem. We've got no costumes," observed Connie.
Michael John squashed the objection with, "Wear your bra and pants and we'll go to the far end of the bay where it's quiet and nobody will be close enough to know the difference. We'd better go to the far end anyhow to keep away from the Lord Lonsdale.

*****

Hours passed in paradise. They alternatively plunged into the almost lukewarm water, so clear that it appeared to have been filtered, and then lay on the virgin white beach tanning. When skin temperatures rose to a certain point they returned to the coolth of the sea. Regularly, they looked up at Antonio's house for a sign. The sun crawled to its zenith. Connie was lying on her back, Bonnie was lying on her stomach teasing a little ghost crab with a strand of wet hair and Michael John was lost in admiration of the two examples of ultimate pulchritude that lay before him. He reluctantly raised his gaze a few degrees and then cried out, "Action stations! The flag is up!'

With that he pulled both Connie and Bonnie to their feet in a single smooth motion and led them up the hill to Antonio's. When they arrived, Antonio was back from his morning's fishing and excitedly handed the radio microphone to Michael John. Bonnie and Connie stood patiently by as a fairly lengthy conversation took place over the air in Portuguese. At last he put the microphone down and turning to the girls said," Our birdies on his way. His truck passed one of Cyprian's OP's about twenty minutes ago. Should be here in about two and half hours. Cyprian seemed disappointed that I didn't want his boys to take Courtney out but I explained it was a matter of personal satisfaction. He understood that. He wishes us luck and would like to see us on the way back to Zimbabwe, eternal optimist that he is!"

"He's going to arrive about three this afternoon and there is no ways we can surprise them on the boat in broad daylight. Shouldn't we take him before he boards and sails away into the blue?" asked Connie.

Michael John replied "No need. We'll stick to our original plan for a night attack. He can't leave much before 11 tonight. I estimate low tide will be at about seven this evening and the Lord Lonsdale will have to wait until just about high tide to clear the coral heads. In the meantime, we can get ready for tonight's work at leisure."

"The Oracle has spoken!" said Connie, partly in fun but partly in admiration at the leadership qualities of the once derelict soldier of fortune.

Michael John moved the Citroen off the road and parked it close to Antonio's house where it wouldn't be seen by Courtney either from the approach to Tofo or from the beach parking area some two hundred metres away. Courtney would not necessarily associate the Citroen with the girls but it might stick out like a sore thumb in a country where half the vehicle population were not roadworthy and the bulk of those that worked, wore the camouflage colouring of the army.

The inflatable raft was checked out for punctures as Antonio had not used it for some time. Michael John spent his time first of all cleaning, checking and oiling the Uzi he had retrieved from under the spare wheel of the Citroen and secondly, in an occupation that bewildered Bonnie who was watching him. He added soot that he had scraped from inside the furnace of Mrs. Antunes's wood burning stove, to half a tin of grease he had scrounged from Antonio. He explained to the watching Bonnie, "Your peaches and cream complexions may be highly acclaimed at the Dorchester in London but will be a dead giveaway against the black of both the dinghy and the sea tonight."

When everything was as ready as they could make it, they sat down to very welcome glasses of cold coconut milk. For the girls it was a unique experience which they enjoyed almost as much as watching Antonio shin up a coconut palm, drop off a couple of coconuts which, when he returned to the ground, he opened with one swift stroke of the large cane knife to reveal the unusual cloudy liquid. They were into their second round of coconut milk when, in the distance they all at once heard the steady drone of an engine. The sound grew louder and then they saw the truck crest the hill and coast down towards the beach parking area below them and toward their left. Examination through the binoculars revealed it to be of Japanese origin, of about eight tonnes capacity and having a large aluminium enclosed body rather like a refrigerated truck.
No sooner had it rolled to a stop when one of the matched pair of blacks climbed from the driver's side of the cab, went around to the other side

and helped a familiar figure down to the ground. The other black had meanwhile alighted and joined his master. Not much more than two hundred metres away, binocular magnification showed Courtney to be obviously hot and disheveled. His skin shone and his cream-coloured suit was creased and sweat stained beneath his arm pits.

Though out of earshot, his moving lips and gesticulating arms indicated that he was giving orders to Narcissus and Adonis who looked somewhat less affected by the long journey and were both dressed in jeans and black T-shirts. Michael John kept glasses fixed on the group and saw Courtney break away and move in the direction of the hotel which he entered, shortly to re-appear again on the sea facing patio. He sank into a chair to loll motionless like a stranded whale. Soon a waiter appeared and placed before him a bottle, glass and ice bucket.

Meanwhile the two blacks had walked down to the water's edge and hauled in by its painter, a red dinghy which had been bobbing up and down in the shallow water just off the shore. They both clambered aboard and one of them plied the oars to take the little boat out to the Lord Lonsdale. They moored the dinghy to the larger boat and clambered aboard only to disappear inside the motor cruiser.

For the best part of twenty minutes nothing happened then the black pair appeared on deck again, climbed into the dinghy and went back to shore. They returned to the truck and opened the back. The inside was not visible to the three observers on the veranda of Antonio's house but the contents of the truck were soon revealed as boxes, crates and large rectangular canvas covered packages were removed from the truck and carried down one or two at a time and then placed carefully in the dinghy. Once the dinghy had sunk well into the water it was rowed back to the Lord Lonsdale and unloaded. This procedure was repeated over and over again. Courtney did not supervise the operation but seemed content to sit in the shade and apply himself to the first bottle and then the one that followed it onto the table.

While others laboured, Connie, Bonnie and Michael John sat quietly and watched intently at first but, once the loading routine was established, only at infrequent intervals. They talked in terms more animated now that their quarry had arrived in the hunting zone. Michael John again took the lead in formulating their plans for that night.
"We should be blessed with some cloud tonight if that lot blows towards us." He pointed to a band of darkish cloud that hovered on the horizon, "wind seems to be right. Anyhow, at about nine o'clock tonight we'll take the dinghy down that path over there which leads over the small promontory you can see to our right and launch it on the other side, well out of sight. We'll paddle out to sea to near the edge of the reef, round the promontory and then travel parallel to the shore until we are opposite Courtney's boat, on the seaside. We should be able to approach safely from there as the sound of the waves breaking on the reef will muffle the sound of our paddles and also, I don't think Courtney will be expecting visitors, especially from the seaside. Sound okay to you?"
"Okay with me," said Bonnie, "but what we do once we are on board?"
Michael John answered the query, "That we will have to play by ear. We will have to overpower them but I have a feeling that we should concentrate on Adonis and Narcissus first as they are obviously fitter and more dangerous than Courtney. I've been thinking just now about what happens when we have dealt with our beauties. I have a strong suspicion that to offload our loot and then hope to cart it safely all the way back through Mozambique, smuggle it through the Zimbabwe Customs and into South Africa is hoping for too much, I have a better plan. Rather let's use the Lord Lonsdale since it is ready for a long trip and I'm sure there would be less risk involved if we were to sail down the coast and put ashore at some quiet spot on the Natal coast of South Africa. I have farming friends in Zululand who will help us hide our booty and then we can dock in Durban with some story of having had to make a run for it from Mozambique. The South African authorities will never know that the boat isn't mine and that it is my means of getting my assets out of Zimbabwe."
"I'll go along with that" said Connie, "but the only thing is that I feel that

we owe a lot to Lucky and Cyprian and if we aren't going to return their way how are we going to reward them for their help?"
"No hassle," continued Michael John, "once we have the boat and its contents secured, we will make a quick trip back to Cyprian's camp. He can have my Citroen and a reasonable sum of Courtney's money. I've decided to make a break with Rhodesia, Zimbabwe or whatever you want to call it and as regards Lucky, I can send documents to him signing over my little house and my other possessions.... don't really mean much to me.... and he'll have enough to set himself up for life."
Bonnie admired the decisiveness of this man and said so.
"Michael John, you angel, you do just that. Make a new start and we'll promise you that you can have as big a chunk of Courtney's fortune as you like, as long as we have enough to get St Mark's off the hook!"
"Agreed!" said Connie.

*****

Time hung heavily on their hands. The time for action was near but the intervening hours passed slowly. As the sun dipped and slowly sank to the horizon, Antonio's wife prepared another meal for them. This time it was chicken peri-peri. The hot spices compensated for the toughness of the bird, witness to its previous athletic ability. Antonio surprisingly, was nowhere to be seen. When Michael John questioned his wife as to his whereabouts, she insisted somewhat unconvincingly that he had gone fishing.
"Unusual," commented Michael John, "the locals are usually scared to death of the sea at night." However, he let the matter rest, and after the meal he picked up a battered guitar, obviously the property of the absent Antonio, tuned it and then accompanied himself in a song, half in Shona and half in English. The words were simple and sad while the accompaniment was a repetition of sombre haunting chords. The words told of a woman crying for her husband who was dead and for her only

son on his way to the war. Connie and Bonnie listened intently and when Michael John stopped, Connie asked him, "Why do you sing such a sad song?"
"It's a song the Selous Scouts always sing before going into action. A habit I suppose, sorry!"
"Don't apologise. It was beautiful." said Bonnie.

Chapter 16

As Michael John had predicted, the clouds rolled in from the sea and obscured the moon. Soon after eight Michael John showed the other two how to smear the soot and grease mixture over the parts of their body which were not covered by their black bra and pants that they wore. He insisted that Bonnie tie her blonde hair up in a black scarf. One of her greatest assets could be a liability on a night such as this. Michael John wrapped the Uzi in a plastic bag which he tied to the belt at his waist. He wore only a dark pair of jeans. When they were ready, he slung the black rubber dinghies, already inflated, onto his back and led the other two from the house whose owner had still not returned. They did not show a light and so their bare feet bore the brunt of the contact with unseen thorns and jagged rocks which lay in the velvet blackness of the night. The sandy path showed dimly and led them towards and then slightly upwards again across the promontory only to dip again to the beach.

Here they launched the dinghy and climbed in. Bonnie and Michael John sat amidships and paddled slowly and steadily out to sea. As they approached the reef's edge the breakers showed massively white and the roar of them breaking was deafening. When the waves seemed about to swamp them, Michael John stroked harder on his side and turned the dinghy parallel to the shore. Soon they rounded the point and could see the lights of Tofo twinkling about a kilometre away to their left. Slowly but surely they gained distance to the north. Michael John estimated that they were roughly halfway to their target. The Lord Lonsdale in its dark blue paint was not visible from where the rubber dinghy rode the swell within the reef, but Michael John had no hesitation in heading inshore when they were slightly past the line of lights which was the hotel Miramar. They slowed the pace now and dipped and lifted the paddles as quietly as possible. Scarcely a sound could be heard as they inched their way inshore. Just as the sea lightened in colour, indicating a sandy, coral free bottom, they saw in outline their target not fifty metres away; not a light showing on board. The bow was pointed towards them as the boat lay with the incoming tide.

They slid the dinghy in silently under the bows and tied up to the anchor chain that hung taut, almost vertically from the boat. Michael John whispered to Connie and Bonnie, unwrapped the Uzi, then worked his way hand over hand up the anchor chain. Where it entered the hull, he stopped and reaching out, grasped the bottom rail of the pulpit and pulled himself up onto the deck. He crept along to crouch in the lea of the deck house while he waited for the other two. They soon joined him and crouched dripping salt water, waiting to make their next move. With infinite patience the three sidled along the port side of the deck house towards the stern. They passed portholes which showed narrow chinks of light coming from the lighted interior. Flush curtains prevented them from looking in.

At the stern end of the wheelhouse, Michael John turned and faced the door that led into the interior of the boat. He stopped and listened, voices came from inside. It seemed that he could hear Adonis and Narcissus. He checked that Bonnie and Connie were close behind him and then, holding the Uzi ready in his right hand, turned the door handle slowly. It turned silently and a little pressure forward indicated that the door was not locked.

Michael John turned to whisper, "Now!" and then threw his weight against the door and as it swung wide stepped inside, the Uzi ready to fire. Behind him Connie and Bonnie entered to stand one on each side of him. The saloon was bathed in light from lamps concealed above the portholes. The whole interior was paneled in sapele mahogany and sumptuously furnished. Padded seats ran the length of the saloon. In the centre stood a long table and at the far end was a bar. Next to the bar was another door, presumably leading to the wheelhouse.

Adonis and Narcissus dressed in one-piece catsuits of some shiny black material sat on stools at the bar. Their heads were turned towards the

interlopers. There was no sign of Courtney.
Michael John was the first to speak, “You two fags raise your hands nice and slowly and step away from the bar.”
The two surprisingly complied immediately, cynical smiles fixed on their faces.
Michael John and his companion stepped further into the saloon and stopped at the edge of the table.
“Frisk them!” instructed Michael John. The girls did so but the pair were clean.
“All right you bastards, where’s your master?”
“Here,” purred a voice from the doorway behind the three.
“Don’t move, whoever you are, you gorgeous looking man, or I’ll spatter your lady friends all over the paneling! Drop that wicked little gun of yours and move away from me!”
The words dripped from Courtney’s lips like venom from a mamba’s fangs.

The Uzi clattered to the ground and Michael John stepped towards his lady friends in the middle of the saloon. He turned to take his first close look at his adversary. Courtney was immaculately dressed in a white sharkskin safari suit and white shoes. In his right hand was an outdated but still fatally effective looking Walther P 38 of Second World War vintage.
He addressed Bonnie and Connie, “My dear girls, you’re hardly dressed for visiting are you?”
His dark little eyes appraise their black grease covered bodies with a homosexual’s lack of interest in the human female form.
“You must introduce me to this lovely friend of yours,” he said looking in the direction of Michael John.
“Stick your fat head up your backside and take a deep breath!” spat Connie.
“Naughty, naughty, little girl.” oozed the sickly smiling animated lump of fat, “so you two won’t give up will you? Attack my property and slaughter my poor guards in a little fit of pique, they tell me. Never mind.

I intended to leave anyway. You only pushed the departure date forward a bit."

Bonnie interrupted the falsetto voice to have her own turn slandering Courtney, "You repugnant slug! You are even lower than the Dead Sea! There should be an open season on you and your kind."
The smile of contempt remained fixed on Courtney's face.
"My dear uninvited guests, you may say what you will but it won't help. It's your misfortune that you insist on interfering with my well laid plans and therefore I must dispense with you. I have to admit that the prospect of your untimely demise gives me a great deal of joy. Before you die of lead poisoning from my dear friend here in my hand, I wish to show you something that will shock you. I wanted to see my modest fortune that is, the part that is readily negotiable. Adonis get out the briefcases!"
Adonis walked behind the bar, bent down and then straightened up again, two large briefcases in his hands. He moved around from the bar and placed them on the large table in view of all.
"Open please !" hissed Courtney.

Adonis worked the locks and opened the cases one after the other to reveal a veritable treasure house. Connie, Bonnie and Michael John could not help gasping at the contents of the cases. The one was packed solid with high denomination notes of at least five different kinds of highly acceptable foreign currency, including British pounds and American dollars. The other contained a tray two centimetres deep filled with emeralds which flashed green fire in the harsh light of the saloon and promised another tray of similar dimensions beneath it.
"Eat your hearts out, you peasants ! That represents only approximately half of my little nest egg. Don't forget the paintings and the objects d'art you once admired so much. They're all on board and will soon grace a lovely chateau which I have my eye on in Lucerne, and now I think we must end our delicious tête-à-tête."

Michael John spoke in a casual collected way, "Mr. Courtney you're

supposed to be a connoisseur of the better things in life. How about you let me have a last King Edward?" With his head, he indicated the cigar box which lay open next to the two briefcases which Adonis had just clicked shut.
"By all means, be my guest. The tides are not quite right yet, so take your time, what little is left."
Bonnie and Connie were wide-awake and caught the cue. They remembered that Michael John had once said how he hated cigars and their aroma. Without making any visible move from where they stood one on each side of the table, they braced themselves for what was to come. Michael John bent casually to reach for a cigar but as his hand hovered over the cigar box, he suddenly made a grab for the nearest briefcase and threw it at Courtney who stood not three metres from him. At the same time, he threw himself after the case in Courtney's direction. In the space of a split second many things happened. Two loud shots rang out and Michael John fell as though poleaxed and Bonnie and Connie sprang round to face the figures that advanced on them.

Adonis moved slowly toward Connie on one side of the table. In his hand had suddenly appeared a long black flick knife which he slashed from side to side in front of the retreating face. Connie stopped moving back as her foot came into contact with the prone figure of Michael John. Adonis saw his chance and lunged forward at her midriff. Connie's left foot was already traveling through the air. The arch of her foot caught the hand that held the knife with such force that the knife dropped harmlessly to the floor. Adonis looked surprised and made to grab her but he was too late. Connie had half turned her left shoulder and then let swing her arm, aided by a twisting motion of her body. The edge of her rigidly extended hand caught Adonis on the point of this nose and drove upwards. It was a well-executed karate chop which first crushed the nasal cartilage and continued to smash bone and drive it up through the nasal sinuses into Adonis's brain. He dropped dead still with the look of astonishment on his face.

On the other side of the table, Narcissus had rushed Bonnie who turned to grab at any weapon. Strong arms shot under her armpits and upwards to lock both hands behind her neck in a full nelson. The hands started to push forward on her neck to bend it beyond the point of no return. At this moment Bonnie blessed the grease that coated her. She raised her arms upwards and dropped smoothly out of Narcissus's grip. As she went down she jerked her right elbow backwards and upwards to deliver an excruciating blow to his groin. Narcissus doubled up and Bonnie turned and straightened him with an accurately delivered knee blow beneath his chin. This arched his face backwards and exposed his throat. Straight fingers jabbed forward and collapsed the C shaped cartilage rings of his windpipe. He sank to the ground grasping for air. Bonnie watched as he struggled to suck oxygen into his lungs and failing to do so slowly died.

Action on both fronts had taken place more or less simultaneously with the result that the two young women gave two contemptuous looks at the dead figures on the floor and in unison turned to survey the rest of the battlefield. Two important facts were immediately evident. First Courtney and the two briefcases had disappeared and secondly Michael John lay deathlike on the floor, blood oozing from the top of his head and from under his arm. He didn't move and Connie cried out, "Michael John! Chioza's prediction. He didn't believe it! "
Both rushed to his side, Connie laid her head on his chest then straightened up and called to Bonnie with relief in her voice, "He's alive!"
To confirm the diagnosis, Michael John stirred, groaned and opened his eyes, his hands moving to clutch his head.
"What the hell happened?" he complained, raising himself to a sitting position. His eyes warily scanned the saloon and took in the two bodies lying about three metres from him.
"Oh Michael John, you're all right and Chioza's all wrong!"
"Sure, I'm okay" he said, his hands gingerly probing his head. "He only creased me and by the feel of it the other shot has missed my ribs but put a furrow in my side. Let's not worry about me. What about

Courtney? Where the hell is he?"
"Skipped by the look of it," answered Connie.
Michael John's brain seemed to have suffered no damage as he spoke to the girls. "He can only have escaped in the boat's dinghy or our inflatable. One way or the other he can't have got far. Above the wheelhouse is a flying bridge and there is a spotlight there. I saw it yesterday through the binoculars. Switch it on and search the sea between here and the shore. Take the Uzi with you and deal with him if he is in range."

Bonnie and Connie both rushed to obey his instructions. They raced into the wheelhouse and up the only gangway leading to the flying bridge. Finding the switch to the spotlight took a little while and then a strong beam of light moved from side to side across the dark, slightly ruffled surface of the water. At last it settled on its desired target. Courtney was paddling slowly and laboriously towards the beach at a point well north of the hotel and at least four hundred metres from the Lord Lonsdale. The range was great but nevertheless Bonnie raised the Uzi and let rip the whole magazine in his direction. Little plumes of water shot up from the sea well short of the dinghy. Courtney did not look round but paddled harder.
"Blast, he's getting away, the bastard" snarled the disappointed Bonnie, wasting valuable time in reloading the Uzi.

The dinghy's bow scraped the sand and Courtney could be clearly seen to snatch a brief case in each hand and swing his left leg over the gunwale into the water. Then, to the watchers astonishment, he leapt into the air. The briefcases flew forwards and landed on the beach. Courtney landed face down, half in and half out of the water and writhed and screamed before he lay still. Bonnie and Connie watched in stunned silence. It was Michael John who had joined them on the fly bridge who broke the silence.
"I think I've got it! The poor bastard stood on a stonefish. They are deadly and lie half buried in the sand in shallow water. You can be sure

he will die and won't enjoy doing it. It's a most painful death."

The light still played on the dinghy and Courtney's body. The searchlight and gunshots had brought no response from the inhabitants of Tofo. Perhaps in these hard times of internal civil war, such nocturnal disturbances represented the norm rather than the exception.

At Michael John's suggestion the girls left him on board and taking the inflatable which still floated safely under the Lord Lonsdale's bows paddled ashore. Examination of Courtney revealed that he was still alive. They hefted, with some difficulty, his body into the dinghy and rowed it back to the Lord Lonsdale. They had not neglected to retrieve the two briefcases. Back on board the girls first tended to Michael John's superficial head wound and the shallow, uncomplicated flesh wound below the shoulder. Antiseptic and plaster sufficed for his head wound and gauze and bandage for the other. A tot of brandy which he labeled as medicinal soon raised Michael John spirits to the level of the two girls. They now turned their attention to Courtney who lay unmoving on a seat in the saloon. At Michael John's suggestion Bonnie searched for and found a well-stocked first aid box. It contained a vial of morphine and a syringe. Bonnie injected the unconscious man. Connie and Bonnie then carried Courtney to a cabin and placed his flaccid body on a bunk. They locked the door.

"If he lives," said Michael John "We'll hand him over to the authorities in South Africa when we get there."
The three sat in the saloon, well pleased with themselves, and made plans for the next day while two bodies lay unmoving in the dinghy anchored to the stern of the bigger boat.

Chapter 17

The three dozed fitfully on the long seats in the saloon and awoke to the shriek of seagulls and a new day's searing sun. They rose, prepared coffee in the neat little galley and then made a tour of inspection of the boat. It was in the engine room that the answer to the question which had puzzled them the night before, the question of how Courtney was expecting them, was solved. Antonio lay securely tied up in the bilge next to one of the large and well maintained Caterpillar diesel engines.

He freely admitted that he had sold them out hoping for a substantial reward from Courtney and now fully expected to be punished for his treachery. Things had turned out too well for Michael John and the girls and enough blood had been spilt, so they packed him into his own boat and sent him on his way with a warning to say nothing to anybody about what had happened in the last two days. He was only too happy to comply.

The inspection of the boat revealed that the packages of valuable objects such as the paintings and Persian rugs had been neatly stacked in two of the boats four cabins. Presumably the unoccupied master cabin was Courtney's and the fourth for the two attendants. The Lord Lonsdale was fitted with extra-large fuel tanks to an estimated capacity of four thousand litres which Michael John calculated should be more than enough for the run to Durban, a distance of approximately one thousand two hundred kilometres. Water tanks were full and the cupboards in the galley were packed with tins of a variety of comestibles. The fridge which was working was stocked with many delicacies such as prawns, squid and sole. Courtney had apparently not intended to suffer any gastronomic discomfort on his flight from Tofo.

As the sun rose higher, Michael John expressed concern for the pre-eminent decomposition of the bodies in the dinghy and the subsequent unpleasant putrefactive contamination of the air around the boat.

Accordingly, he climbed down into the dinghy, rearranged its human cargo and plied the oars to send the small craft slowly out towards the reef. From Antonio's house he had seen and mentally marked a break in the reef. It was towards the gap that he was headed. Waves surged through the gap and threatened to swamp the dinghy but he put his back into rowing and slowly the dinghy inched through into the deeper and less choppy water beyond. Well away from the breakers he swung south for a short distance and shipped the oars. He tied a length of chain to each body and then levered them on to the gunwale and over into the azure blue sea. The bodies sank silently downwards, their passage marked by bubbles escaping from the folds of clothing, forced out and up as pressure increased. The water was too deep to see their final resting places, temporary as they were to be; the Mozambique sharks being no less voracious than their brethren elsewhere.

Back on the Lord Lonsdale Michael John prepared to leave the girls for the journey back to Cyprian's camp. He had decided to go on his own and leave the girls on board to rest and relax prior to the long sea voyage ahead.

"I don't think that I will make it back today - not enough hours of light left so don't panic if I get back sometime tomorrow morning." were his parting words as he set off for the beach in the dinghy.

*****

The afternoon was unbearably hot on the boat and the girls stripped off several times and dived into the crystal clear water. They found a couple of facemasks and snorkels in a locker in the saloon and once they got the hang of using them could not drag themselves away from the marine wonderland they discovered. They floated on their fronts with masked heads facing downwards so long that they were forced to clamber back aboard and cover their bodies with pants and shirts as a protection against the sun, before returning to their newly found and delightful pastime.

They discovered that nature had endowed the denizens of the brine with colours so brilliant and varied as to make the most vivid land animal drab by comparison. They drifted with the tide over coral colonies of a dozen different shapes, brain and antler horn amongst them. Each coral head was home to a myriad of little fish, cheeky brown, yellow and white clownfish, electric blue wrasses with long slender, laterally compressed bodies, graceful Moorish idols in a livery of silver white and black and yellow, like distorted plates sporting fins which looked more for show than the locomotion; and thousands more.

They also saw the devils of the deep; the vicious looking moray eels who lurked, heads protruding, in underwater caverns. Barely moving black pin cushions which were sea urchins and the scorpion fish, multihued with numerous poisonous spines, first cousin to the stone fish which had objected to Courtney's heavy foot.

With skin wrinkled by long contact with the water and backs and legs burnt bright red by the merciless sun, they at last went back on board. Supper that night was a quiet affair in the absence of Michael John and they soon surrendered to Morpheus aided by the rocking of the boat on the incoming tide and the lullaby of the wavelets that lapped along the hull of the vessel.

Again, day dawned to a clear sky and burning sun. Connie erected a canvas shelter over part of the aft deck and sat dreamily in a deck chair. From time to time she played a pair of binoculars on the beach and was doing just that when she saw the white Citroen pull to a stop in the beach car park. A familiar figure climbed out and then waved to whoever drove off in his car.
"Michael John's back!" called Connie through the open door of the

saloon. This brought tousle-haired Bonnie rushing out on the deck. Even as he dragged himself over the deck rail the barrage of questions started. "Did you have any problems? Is Cyprian happy with what you gave him? Who drove you back here?" came from Connie.
"Did you send the letter to Lucky? Do you think that Cyprian will make sure it gets to him?" from Bonnie.
"Whoa girls!" said a smiling Michael John, "let me tell you the whole story. The trip back to the camp was totally uneventful. Cyprian was there and delighted to see me and to hear about what happened to Courtney and his mates. He did say however, that he could have saved us a lot of time by ambushing them on the road in his territory. I had to emphasize that it was a job we wanted to do ourselves. He was highly pleased with the offer of the car and the money. He sent one of his minions in civvies to bring me back and take the car. As for the letter to Lucky, I made another copy which I gave to Cyprian to post at Mavanza or Nhachenque and the original, I posted myself in Maxixe. One is sure to get through to our friend and his mother's days of poverty should be over. Right! Have I covered everything?"
"I suppose so. But you haven't said how much you missed us!" pouted Bonnie.
Michael John did not answer but swept her into his arms and kissed her so long and deeply that Connie yelled, "Time! "and swapped places with Bonnie. When at last they separated, Michael John caught his breath before he said: "Right it's all systems go for South Africa now. I once did a course in navigation and though it was on land it shouldn't be too difficult at sea. The way I see it is that we must plot a course to take just far enough out to sea to avoid any reefs or government patrol boats but not so far that we can't get back in shore if a storm blows up. There are only two things stopping us from leaving right this minute. Firstly, it wouldn't be wise to leave in broad daylight. Somebody in Tofo might phone the port authorities and in Inhambane who will come down on us like a ton of bricks for leaving without being officially cleared and the other thing is that the tide is wrong. We won't clear the coral heads on the way to the gap in the reef unless it is almost full tide. About eleven

tonight everything should be perfect for our departure. In the meantime, I'm thirsty for a cold drink and also you two.

The line fisherman in the dugout canoe was too engrossed in earning his livelihood to take any notice of the muffled sounds of enmeshed bodies that drifted from the cabin on the shimmering heat haze to where he fished not one hundred metres from the Lord Lonsdale.

*****

In the wheelhouse, Michael John pressed first one starter button and then the other and grunted happily as the deep throb of the twin diesels reverberated through the whole boat. He yelled to Connie in the bows, "Raise anchor!" and as the winch did its work and the dark shining chain piled up on the deck, he spun the spokes of the ships wheel until the illuminated compass showed the reading he wanted. Not a light burned on board and the night had a glassy stillness. He eased the twin throttles forward and thrilled at the forward thrust the boat gave as the bow lifted. At less than half speed they headed towards the reef.

Connie who stood beside him in the wheelhouse asked, "How do you know where the gap is? Aren't you going too fast?"
"Lover, trust me. This afternoon I took a compass bearing on the gap and that's the way we are pointed now." replied Michael John, as he adjusted the wheel a fraction.

Connie joined the other two and for five minutes the boat slid smoothly over the surface of the sea, visible only in places where small waves broke in excited abandon as if involved in an intimate love affair with the pockets of wind that danced across them. At close hand the gap in the reef was plainly visible, breakers to the left and right and nothing in between. The power of the diesels was more than a match for the tide race and with little more than a slight yawing motion, they were through to the open sea.

The drum of the engine increased to a deep throated roar as Michael John eased the throttles further forward. Gently he turned the wheel round clockwise and the speeding vessel turned in a wide circle to the east. For twenty minutes they continued on this bearing until Michael John judged it time to alter the course again to the starboard, this time to a bearing of due South.

Once on the southward reach towards Cabos dos Correntos, everything at eye level and below was engulfed in an inky blackness. Only the heavens showed it's individuality, emphasized by the stars that twinkled as they shed light towards the earth eagerly before being shadowed out by clouds. Not even the lights of Tofo were any longer visible. The surface of the sea was almost unruffled but the boat settled into a slow corkscrew motion formed by the heavy swell that swept unhindered from the north-east towards the shore.

For two more hours, they ran smoothly through the night with not a single miss from the engines that roared beneath them. The air was getting quite cold and so Bonnie went down to the galley to make coffee while Connie took a turn at the wheel. Michael John peered in the direction of the invisible land on their starboard and again judged it time to change course.
"Bring her to a bearing of South, South West," he told Connie and she hesitatingly complied. She raised her eyes from the binnacle and looked through the windscreen in front of her.
"Michael John" she said, "there is a light ahead, slightly to the right of us. What is it?"
Before answering, Michael John switched on the torch and shone it on the chart open on the table behind Connie. Within less than a minute he was able to give his answer. "It must be Ponta Zavora, but there's no lighthouse marked on the chart. Maybe it is new and the chart is old. Just

stick to the bearing and keep an eye on the light."

There was silence for a few minutes and then Connie said: "that light is moving or else I'm going mad. Lighthouses don't move!"
In answer to this statement Michael John picked up the binoculars and scanned the forward horizon.
"Bloody hell! It's a boat and a fast moving one at that. It's coming straight at us!" he mouthed angrily.
"What boat, whose boat?" cried Connie.
"I don't know but there is a horrible possibility that it is a government patrol boat and if it is, that's bad news. They're Russian-made, well-armed and faster than we are, or so I have read."
"But how can they see us from that distance?" queried Connie.
"They can't but they have got radar." came the reply. He continued, "Give me the wheel and in case it is what we think it is, get down below and get the two briefcases. Then this is what you must do. Get a claw hammer or something similar and use it to carefully lever a couple of planks from that life raft on the aft deck. Wrap the briefcases in some canvas, slide them into the hollow centre of the life raft and then carefully nail back the planks. Whatever happens, if it is a patrol boat, they won't, hopefully, get hold of the most precious part of our cargo. Assuming nothing of a permanently unpleasant nature happens to us, we may get a chance to retrieve them."

As Connie left to do what had been asked, Bonnie arrived with the coffee. The coffee was destined to grow cold in the cups for no sooner had Michael John appraised Bonnie of the situation than a shot rang out from the now fast closing and recognizable patrol boat and a plume of water shot up in front of the bows of the Lord Lonsdale. Michael John scarcely hesitated before he cut the twin diesels and switched on the riding lights.

Chapter 18

The patrol boat rapidly closed the distance between them. A blindingly bright searchlight located and shone persistently on three dejected persons who stood on the deck. With a very un-naval-like manoeuvre, the patrol boat made violent contact with the Lord Lonsdale. Scruffy uniformed men leapt from the patrol boat and secured the two vessels together. An officer, judging by his jauntily perched cap, stepped aboard the Lord Lonsdale and addressed Michael John and the two girls in Portuguese. Of the three only Michael John had any idea as to what was being said and accordingly, when the officer paused, gave them the gist of it.

"This gentleman is Capitao Jardim of the Mozambique Navy. He is placing us under arrest for trying to leave the country illegally and has confiscated the boat. I complained that we hadn't left the county as we were still within territorial waters but he says it doesn't matter as we were obviously going to try to duck out since we did not receive official clearance when we left Tofo. We're going to be taken back to Maxixe pending our transportation to Maputo for trial. I guess we're in a right royal mess this time!"

Before what Michael John had said had been fully digested by Connie and Bonnie, a sailor rushed up to the captain and jabbered away in Portuguese. The captain's voice was even sterner than before as he addressed Michael John. Michael John replied protesting but the captain silenced him almost immediately. Michael John turned to the girls and explained the new development

"One of his men has found the goodies in the cabin and now we're being accused of smuggling valuables out of this country. I tried to explain that the bloody stuff was not of Portuguese origin but this Gilbert and Sullivan character shut me up."

"Oh hell ! We're for it now!" complained Bonnie.

"I don't fancy the idea of a prison in this primitive state. Is there no way

out, Michael John?" asked Connie.
"If you're thinking of bribing this lot with the money and/or the emeralds, forget it. Why should they let us go if we reveal where they are hidden when they could have the lot and us both for the asking? We'll just have to go along with what this bunch of thugs want and hope that a chance to escape presents itself. Meanwhile let's put on a brave face and not give them the satisfaction of thinking we are intimidated." said Michael John with somewhat less than his usual amount of exuberance.

The captain gave orders and the three were marched across a makeshift gangplank to the patrol boat and locked in what appeared to be a paint locker. The solid steel door slammed shut and cut off most of the light. What little light did find its way through the grime on the glass of the one and only porthole revealed that they would have to share their accommodation with an untidy collection of tins of paint of various colours and volumes.

Michael John tried to open the porthole but the locking bolts were corroded solid, witness to the singular lack of brass and elbow grease on this particular naval vessel. The smell of turps increased and then leveled out at an extremely uncomfortable concentration.

A dull rumble between beneath them indicated engines in operation and judging by the rather uncomfortable corkscrew motion of the vessel, they were headed forward at an angle to the swell and therefore on their way back to Maxixe or Inhambane. Each of the occupants selected a good-sized paint tin and sat on it. They discussed their present situation and agreed that to try and escape at sea was hazardous if not impossible. They tried to cheer each other up with suggestions as to the situations that could arise once ashore and which might present a chance to get out of the clutches of Frelimo.

By wiping the porthole glass with a paint rag, they were able to see that the day was dawning as the engines slowed and the patrol boat lost way. From the porthole they could see that they were running up the wide estuary between Inhambane on the port side and Maxixe on the starboard side. The town of Inhambane and its wooden pier were clearly visible as the boat started to make a wide swing to the starboard to bring it up facing seawards against the jetty below the town of Maxixe. The docking manoevre was done with such a lack of skill that the hard bump that indicated the successful conclusion of the move shook the occupants of the paint locker.

*****

The sunlight was blinding as they were marched at gunpoint from the dockside up a sloping stone-surfaced road in the direction of the town. Crowds looked on in interested silence. They did not have far to march before they came to an old stone building with a castellated parapet and iron grilles over each window. It had once been a Portuguese fortress dating back to the sixteenth century and now the local jail and Frelimo headquarters. The bearded and relatively smart Capitao handed over his charges to the Frelimo Comandante whose tailor was obviously in liquidation as all that he wore was a peaked cap, patched trousers of faded olive green and boots whose uppers were in the process of parting company with the soles. The three were forced to stand and listen to a long conversation between the two members of the armed forces. The captain's widely waving hands and sound effects as he described what had probably been his one and only naval action, were highly descriptive.
When he had finished, the Frelimo officer dressed his three prisoners in broken English.
"You spies! You South Africans! You stay here in my prison then you go to Maputo when I am able. No try run away or I shoot you, bang bang!"
"And a Merry Christmas to you." said Connie.

“Careful, don’t anger the general, he might blow a valve.” cautioned Bonnie.

The officer turned to one of his minions and gave him instructions. The minion gesticulated with his AK. And marched the three down a long, dark passage which opened into a room in which three Frelimo soldiers in various states of undress played cards on the table next to an ashtray full of cheroot stubs. The soldiers paused in their card play long enough to watch Michael John, Connie and Bonnie being locked in one of the cells that flanked three sides of the room.

The accommodation was so bad as to make the paint locker seem like a luxury hotel suite. On the floor was scattered some dry and obviously very old straw. In one corner was a bucket that exuded such a foul stench as to leave no doubt as to its function. The only other thing in the cell was a narrow wooden slatted bed on which reposed a coir mattress which was disgorging it’s stuffing from a dozen different holes.
“I suppose we can’t complain, the tariff is very reasonable” quipped Bonnie, pinching her nose firmly between thumb and forefinger.
“This place makes an Arab’s armpit seem like paradise” said Connie, also blocking her nasal passages.

Michael John seemed oblivious of the dirt and smell as he carefully surveyed their surroundings. He conveyed the result of his survey to the others.
“The walls are about a metre thick, the bars on the window has stood for four hundred years and not yielded to internal pressures and the same applies to the door. I don’t see any way out. We’ll have to wait and see what happens.”

At about midday, a soup of cabbage floating in greasy water and accompanied by a small bowl of mealie pap was brought to them. The bearer of the culinary disaster was well covered by the card playing soldiers - no chance to escape. Three helpings of food went into the bucket in the corner.

In the late afternoon, two guards came in to take them to a small office with a small desk in the middle at which sat a very well-dressed black in a dark suit, white shirt and subdued tie. He was about thirty years old and with his thin moustache and dark glasses reminded the girls of a typical London spiv.

He spoke in a low but forceful tone in Portuguese. Michael John had to again translate for the benefit of the others.
"He is the local commissar. He says we will get at least ten years each for smuggling, that is if we ever get a trial. The boat and all our possessions will be confiscated. He is offering us an easier way out. If we are prepared to sign confessions that we are South African spies, he will ensure a quick trial and a token sentence of say two years. The boat and goodies still stay behind. I don't trust him, I think he's just trying to generate some propaganda against South Africa."

"I have never been in any part of the world where two parties, the so-called frontline states and South Africa are so neurotic about each other. I'm not prepared to be part of it at any price. He can go to hell!" declared Connie.

Michael John and Bonnie agreed and the former turned to the commissar and delivered their decision. The commissar's voice rose and he ranted and raved at them for a good two minutes before ordering the guards to return them to their cell.

*****

There were no more interruptions before nightfall. Stars appeared in the high barred opening which was the only window to the cell and muffled sounds of an animated gambling and drinking session could be heard through the iron door. At nine o'clock one of the guards opened the cell door and placed on the floor an old wine demi-john full of tepid water. Since they had had nothing to drink for the better part of twenty hours the three were parched and disposed of the contents of the bottle within a minute.

The grass on the floor did not provide a comfortable bed but was preferable to the dirty coir mattress and so the three settled down to try and sleep. Eventually they did fall asleep only to be woken by the sound of thunder. Michael John looked out of the high window and then said: "Very funny, it's two o'clock in the morning, the sky is clear, judging by the stars I can see and yet I can hear thunder."
The rumbles of thunder grew louder and more frequent which prompted Connie to say; "I don't suppose you two are thinking what I'm thinking. Clear skies and thunder, that sounds as if we are in the middle of a ruddy civil war!"
As if to clarify the matter, automatic rifle fire was now clearly audible.
"Oh lummy" moaned Bonnie, "I'm getting a bit tired of bangs. Can't Cyprian and his friends go fight somewhere else?"
"It might well be Cyprian and his lot and hopefully it is. We're reasonably safe behind the stout walls. Short of a rocket straight through the window, we're okay for the duration." said Michael John.

Wide awake now, Michael John and the girls could do nothing more than listen to the progress of the battle, highlighted now and again by the flashes of light visible in the high opening of the window. A couple of loud explosions rocked even the massive building in which they were incarcerated. These were followed by the distinct sound of automatic fire within the building which got closer and closer.

The demise of the card players outside the cell door was a deafening affair and the iron of their door suddenly seem flimsy. One stray bullet did penetrate the door and whining over Bonnie's head, embedded itself in the wall opposite. The firing died down and the opening of cell doors could be heard. Finally, their turn came as the door was thrown open by a wild eyed, heavily armed group of men dressed in camouflage. Their spokesman spoke Portuguese but there was no mistaking the gist of what he said; they were free, like all the other prisoners who milled around the guards anteroom. A relieved trio thanked their rescuers and trooped down the passage out into the moonlit street.

Sporadic fighting was still taking place in the distance but not in their section of the town. Frelimo were conspicuous by their absence. Michael John suggested that, without exposing themselves unnecessarily, they should make their way down to the harbour and if the boat was still there and fit to sail, they should make their second attempt to leave this beautiful but troubled part of the world.

In the shadows of the buildings that lined the streets, they worked their way carefully downwards towards where they had last seen the Lord Lonsdale. They could see the boat safely secured to the jetty not one hundred metres away, when a body of rebels, or so they supposed them to be, rounded a corner and approached them up the street. The leader was speaking into a radio handset that there was no mistaking the short, stocky figure. It was Cyprian.

He came up to them grinning, "We meet again! One of my soldiers told me that among the prisoners he released were two white women and a man. I knew it must be you." He hugged Michael John and politely shook hands with the two women with the comment, "You three are harder to get rid of than mopani flies!"

Disengaging himself from the bigger man he went on, "Your boat is safe and sound, but I've heard that the day it was docked, a lot of crates were removed and taken into the town somewhere. Perhaps you want me to

get my men to make a quick search? We're pulling out in about an hour. We're not yet in a strong enough position to hold the town but have done Frelimo a lot of damage tonight."
The last sentence was uttered with a widening grin.
"Buddy," said Michael John, "don't worry about looking for Courtney's treasure. I reckon we should get the hell out of here while the going is good. Hopefully, Frelimo didn't find part of the loot we stashed away on the Lord Lonsdale."
"My friend we shall say goodbye again. Perhaps we will meet again in another war in another place at another time." With this Cyprian clasped Michael John's hand with both of his, nodded to Bonnie and Connie and walked away up the street followed by his small party of rebels.
"That man always seems to pop up at the right time." commented Connie as they walked down to the quayside.

The Lord Lonsdale bobbed gently up and down on the incoming tide. Michael John made straight for the wheelhouse and breathed a sigh of relief when the twin diesels fired at the first push of the starter buttons. Bonnie meanwhile, unable to control her impatience, had rushed to the stern to find the life raft. It was where they left it She yanked with all her might at one of the planks that had been nailed back the night before and saw the two briefcases still nestling safety in the hollow of the raft. She conveyed the good news to Connie who was just then casting off the forward mooring line prior to jumping across the narrow gap on to the already moving Lord Lonsdale.

Chapter 19

Michael John's eyes lit up as he saw the briefcases. He slowly spun the wheel and the boat edged its way out at half speed towards the centre of the wide creek. Soon the lights of Maxixe supplemented by the glow of burning buildings lay astern to the port side and the lights of Inhambane astern to the starboard.

As they gained the open sea, the same heavy swell of the previous night was still running. The Lord Lonsdale laboured slightly up each swell and then raced down into the trough beyond. The engines were running at full power and the boat was making about fifteen knots into the wind.

It was Michael John who broke the silence in the wheel house.
"This time we'll try a different tack. We'll head out to sea, a respectable distance, before turning south. You have to take a chance on my navigation; we'll be well into the shipping lanes. Sneaking down the coast didn't work, so maybe a more brazen approach will. We will have to switch on the navigation lights or we could end up examining barnacles on the underside of some Liberian tanker. Okay?"
"I agree" said Connie
"So, do I" said Bonnie and she added, "if you can plot a course for us, we can take turns at the wheel. You can't do all the driving, Michael John."
Michael John laughed at the un-nautical use of the term "driving" but agreed to the suggestion with the proviso that he would stay on watch until they were well out to sea and set on a southerly course.

At about one in the morning and land astern, Michael John altered course to due south. All was silent except the continual sound of the bow cutting through the water, throb of the diesels and the curling of the twin waves of the wake. The land lay over the horizon and the only light came from the fading moon, the persistent stars above and the twin lights of red and green glowing on the masthead. Michael John felt disinclined to awaken the girls who now were asleep soundly below and so he stayed at the wheel.

Shortly before dawn a ships lights were visible on the port horizon and the sight of them jogged Michael John into full consciousness and the realisation that he had been dozing. Fatigue was now closing in on him, so he locked the wheel and went below to call Bonnie who made a cup of hot coffee for each of them before taking over from Michael John who was asleep within seconds of stretching his body out on the bunk.

*****

"What a fantastic day" thought Michael John as he came up the companionway onto the deck. It was ten in the morning; the sky was cloudless and a deep blue that indicated considerable depth. A steady breeze blew and raised white horses which white flecked the sea stretching as far as they could see. The occasional flying fish rose out of the water, skimmed over the surface and then resigned to the inevitability of the pull of gravity, sank back into its natural habitat. Bonnie lay naked on a towel on the deck near the stern and turned her head to greet Michael John. Connie was at the wheel, happily munching on an apple. Michael John crept up behind her and before she could protest at had slid his hands under the T-shirt and grasped her breasts. Connie sighed contentedly and nuzzled the stubble covered face that rested next to hers.
"Oh, Michael John, it's so peaceful after last night isn't it? It's like being on a luxury cruise. I wish it could go on forever...... no stop to it!" This she said as teeth nibbled at the lobe of her ear.
"Maybe things are going right for us now. Perhaps we can just lie back and enjoy the trip. Want me to take the wheel for a bit?" said Michael John.
"No, I only took over from Bonnie an hour ago. Why don't you go and join her? I can't concentrate on seduction and navigation at the same

time!" answered Connie.
"Fine! I know when I'm not wanted!" Michael John said as he playfully smacked the rump that protruded cheekily out of a minute pair of tanga pants. He left to join Bonnie.

Shortly before midday, Michael John stopped ogling Bonnie to return to the wheelhouse to dig out Courtney's sextant. He took a noon sight and set hunched over the chart for some minutes. Assuming that the chronometer, that was mounted on the wall above the chart table was correct, he calculated the position to be 26° 15 min south and 33° 30 min East. He looked up from the chart and said to Connie who was still at the wheel, "We're going great guns if my calculations are correct. We have actually passed Maputo and are about fifty kilometres off Ponta Abril. We seem to be drifting slightly to the West though, so you better correct course to a bearing of 175°.... can't risk running aground, at least until we're sure that the ground isn't Mozambique. We should be in South African waters by about three o'clock this afternoon."
Connie's reply was to leave the wheel just long enough to hug Michael John and tell him, "You really are the mostest you know!".
"Lock the wheel on a course of 175 degrees and let's go down, collect Bonnie and rustle up some lunch." said Michael John, reddening rapidly.

"Ye gods, this is the life!" said Bonnie leaning back against a cushion and sipping at a glass of chilled Veuve Cliquot 57 from Courtney's comprehensive stock of select wines.
"Mmmm, that crayfish went down a treat." agreed Connie.
"Well, if our inner selves are now satisfied, I think we must carefully plan our next move." suggested Michael John, "The easiest place for us to slip ashore is the St Lucia estuary. There's enough depth in the Mfolozi river mouth and also, more important, the Lord Lonsdale won't be particularly noticeable there. Lots of rich farmers and business tycoons have biggish boats moored there or they call in from their fishing trips. The other thing is that my former friend Tony Marshall has this farm near Matubatuba only about thirty kilometres from St Lucia." He paused

for a moment, doing a mental calculation before carrying on "again, according to my calculations, we will be off St Lucia at about two o'clock tomorrow morning. To enter then would not be a good idea ...a bit suspicious arriving at that time of the morning. What we will do is wait until I think we're out of Mozambique waters, say about four o'clock this afternoon and then reduce speed to seven knots, half speed, I reckon. This should get us to St Lucia in the late afternoon tomorrow. We'll enter the estuary at last light, I'll get to Tony somehow to arrange safe keeping of the briefcases and we can leave at first light and make for Durban."
"You're the boss." Teased Bonnie as she emptied her champagne glass, and carried on to say, "while we are all three here together, I think it's high time we open the briefcases and count the money to see what we have got."
"Great!" said Connie, "what a marvelous job to do, counting money knowing it's ours!"

Michael John retrieved the briefcases and counting started. They each selected a particular foreign currency and having counted it wrote the total on a piece of paper. When they'd finished they racked their brains to remember what the exchange rate for a particular currency was. When eventually they agreed on a figure, Michael John did the required conversions until he had a neat column of figures as English pounds. He added these and rechecked before stating in a highly satisfied one, "I make it two and a quarter of a million pounds, give or take a bit of error in exchange rates."
"That's absolutely perfect. That's enough to give Max his money, pay our debts and that includes you Michael John and Jannie. We won't have a clue as to what the emeralds are worth but at least they'll fetch enough to give us some working capital with plenty over for the orphanage." enthused Bonnie. With this she left to go on watch.

Connie and Michael John also rose to go to the master cabin, taking with them the unfinished bottle of champagne. As they entered the cabin Connie said wickedly, "We'll finish what you started in the wheelhouse this morning!"

*****

The weather continued perfect that afternoon, though of the three only Bonnie was aware of it. Michael John looking tousled and freshly showered, relieved her of the wheel at about five. A tanker passed to port as the sun slid down towards the horizon. Michael John switched on the navigation lights and sat in the semidarkness, staring at the compass that glowed in the binnacle. For the first time he was emotionally aware of the break he had had to make with the land of his birth. He consoled himself that perhaps the sadness was the sadness that comes after making love. He could not however, chase from his mind the visions of the veld and the mountains, the drought and the rains, the blue jacarandas and the autumn hued msasas of the country he had left behind. He was glad to leave his post, having checked that there were no ships lights visible and join the other two in the saloon

Courtney's larder provided another sumptuous meal, this time washed down with a refreshing semi-sweet Lagosta, a wine from Portugal. After they had sated themselves, Connie took the next watch but not before Michael John had instructed her that, if she saw any ships lights approaching, unless they were well on the starboard bow, she was to turn to the starboard so as to pass port side to port side. He also reiterated that a red light was for port and a green for starboard or left and right if she preferred it that way.

The wine and the good food had restored Michael John's spirit and strength, so that Bonnie was extremely disappointed when her turn came at eleven to change places with Connie. At the change of watch Michael John went with Bonnie to the wheelhouse to change the course

185° to keep parallel with the shore which now angled slightly to the west of south. As it happened a ship's lights were visible ahead and Michael John watched as Bonnie confidently turned the boat starboard and then back on to course once the large vessel had passed safely by.

At three in the morning, Bonnie stamped hard on the deck to rouse a now very exhausted but happy Michael John to relieve her. The presence of low cloud on the horizon made the dawn as spectacular a one as Michael John had ever seen. The clouds became shot with shades of pink and purple and the sea looked like a rough layer of molten gold. Seagulls swooped over the boat as a reminder that the coast was not that far to the west.

The wind increased in velocity and raised waves that tumbled in the same direction as the boat and made the going uncomfortable. The boat was now rising and sinking over a vertical distance of about six metres. Not one of the three was actually seasick but the motion of the boat in conjunction with the cloudy sky conditions did not make for as pleasant cruising as the previous day. At noon a gap in the clouds allowed Michael John to get a genuine shot of the sun from which he calculated their position as being approximately twenty kilometres off Mission Rocks on the Zululand Coast. This meant that at the present rate they would reach St Lucia too early. Accordingly, Michael John reduced speed further to the extent that the waves were overtaking them. He also altered course towards shore. As he did so, he was a little surprised to hear the drone of a light aircraft again. The thought flashed through his mind that it might somehow be Courtney on their trail but he dismissed this idea as impossible.

Just before five in the afternoon, the coast, lined with golden beaches and fringed with casuarina trees, was clearly visible and not long afterwards the break in the line of dunes showed the mouth of a large river. It was just getting dark as Lord Lonsdale put into the river and anchored half a kilometre upstream.

In all three the desire to place their feet safely back on terrafirma was strong and so by mutual agreement they decided to have an evening meal ashore. Delivery of the briefcases to Tony could wait until the next day. Michael John suggested a restaurant in St Lucia, the town itself being about a kilometre from the river. Accordingly, they showered and dressed aboard before setting off for the riverbank in the ships dinghy. A lift into town was no problem as many fishermen were coming ashore after a day's fishing and heading in their cars and beach buggies, back to the hotels and holiday accommodation in town. The Afrikaner farmer who gave them a lift was fishless, sunburnt but full of high spirits.

Their dinner was adequate if nothing else and the evening cool enough for the three to enjoy the walk back to the river. They strolled along the casuarina lined shore and then inland along the riverbank to where they had left the dinghy. Bonnie and Connie climbed in and Michael John was just about to push the dinghy into deeper water when a brilliant flash of orange light lit up the whole of the lower reaches of the river. A split second later the sound of the explosion with its accompanying shockwaves hit them.

They looked instinctively in the direction of the explosion and saw to their horror that it was the Lord Londsdale which had exploded. The remains of the boat was burning furiously and pieces of debris that had been flying skywards were now falling in the water not far from where they stood.
The three stood riveted where they were and for some seconds not one of them spoke, even after the sound of the explosion had died down.
"I don't believe it was an accident." said Michael John. "I have seen a small plane flying over the boat on two occasions on the way down the coast. Somehow I think Courtney must have got away during the Renamo attack and has conned someone into lending him a plane to keep tracks on us."

Bonnie suggested, "And while we were ashore it looks like he went on board, probably found the briefcases and set an explosive charge on a time fuse. I suppose he daren't take the boat itself and didn't want us to have it. Oh, sod it!"

The theories that had had been advanced to explain the events of the last few minutes seemed destined to be verified at least in part as Connie gazed along the bank towards the sea only to see a figure of familiar dimensions clambering into a car not more than four hundred metres away. In the semidarkness it was just possible to make out the two pieces of luggage that he flung into the back of the car.
"It's him!" Connie gossiped and pointed for the benefit of the other two.
"Good Lord it is, and about to do a disappearing act again!" cried Bonnie

Michael John wasted no words but ran to a beach buggy parked close by. He reached in and felt along the dashboard. With relief he located the ignition keys.
"Move it you two!" he yelled as he swung into the driving seat and switched on. The engine fired, missed and then started. Connie and Bonnie had thrown themselves into the vehicle. Michael John revved the engine and let out the clutch so violently that the back wheels sent up sprays of gravel before they dug in and the beach buggy shot forward.

The tail lights of Courtney's vehicle were just disappearing around the first bend in the coast road. The beach buggy sped after it. Courtney was no slouch as a driver and the Peugeot he drove was soon hitting a hundred and twenty kilometres an hour as it headed north along a winding ribbon of tar which twisted one way and then the other through the avenue of casuarinas. Michael John drove like a demon, taking the beach buggy to the limit on each and every corner. Lacking the top speed of the Peugeot, the beach buggy was not gaining any ground. Tyres screeched and the two vehicles rocked dangerously on every corner for more than three kilometres. Courtney's brake lights came on suddenly as the beach road ended in a T-junction. Without stopping, the Peugeot turned right. The beach buggy slackened off speed even less at the junction and gained a bit on the car in front. Along a straight, narrow strip of tar the two cars sped at breakneck speed.

Suddenly the occupants of the vehicle behind saw brake lights again and Courtney's car braked hard, slewed to one side and came to a violent stop against two large gates which closed the road. Courtney extracted himself from the car, hastily retrieved the briefcases from the back of the car and after having examined the gates cursorily, turned away and ran down a side road nearby.

By the time the beach buggy came to a halt at the gates which, according to the sign, closed the entrance to a game park, there was no sign of Courtney. Michael John and the two women jumped out of the beach buggy and started down the side road which Courtney had taken. Fifty metres further on, they ran under an arch which carried a sign that read 'Crocodile Park' but which they did not see. They scrambled over a small locked gate and gained on Courtney, handicapped as he was by his bulk. They soon saw him running and slipping down a grassy bank towards a small dam. The trio followed at full tilt.

Instead of running around the dam, Courtney made for a narrow bridge that spanned the water. His speed lessened as he waddled over the cross planks of the bridge, the brief cases slowed him down as they snagged, time and time again, against the uprights of the handrails on either side. He stopped, gasping, in the middle of the bridge trying to catch his breath. The wood of which the bridge had been made was not perhaps of the best quality when it had been constructed. Any lack in quality had been compounded by the years of standing in the sun and rain. It was not surprising that the two laths which Courtney stood on cracked, then broke noisily in the middle. Courtney screamed and dropped the briefcases behind him. His large body fell through the hole created by the broken planks. He slipped down until he managed to grab hold of the two longitudinal members with his hands. His soft hands battled to maintain a handhold while his gross body dangled below the bridge.

Michael John and the girls pulled up on the grassy bank before the bridge. Other than Courtney's screams, they heard other sounds and saw long, low, dark bodies slithering turbulently into the water from the bank to their right. They saw the bow waves made by the snouts of the beasts as they cruised towards the sound of Courtney's screeches.

A large head surfaced below Courtney, reached up and snapped at his feet. Courtney screamed fit to awaken the dead as he bent his knees in an effort to raise his feet from the gaping mouth of the four metre long monster. This infuriated the crocodile which backed down into the water and then lunged upwards with all its might. Bending legs didn't help and huge jaws with their opposite facing rows of saw-like teeth, closed on one leg. The onlookers distinctly heard the sound of tooth on bone. The crocodile tried to drop back into the water with its prey but Courtney hung on. He no longer screamed but used every ounce of his strength to keep his fingers curled about the two pieces of wood they clung to.

Slowly his fingers uncurled and suddenly his grip was broken. The reptilian monster pulled him under with a mighty splash. Three more crocodiles joined the first to fight for a share of the prey. The water under the bridge churned and boiled as jaws snapped and tails lashed. All of a sudden it was over as each reptile took its share of the meal to its own feeding place. The last visible sign of Hartley de Vere Courtney was the stain of his blood that showed black against the grey of the night darkened water.

Connie and Bonnie clutched Michael John, burying their heads in his shoulders and shivered uncontrollably.

Chapter 20

Back at the beach buggy they pondered their predicament. All their personal belongings had gone with the Lord Lonsdale. The demise of the boat could not have gone unnoticed by the local population and consequently the local constabulary. On the credit side they still had the briefcases intact and luckily their passports which Bonnie had placed in her handbag when they came ashore.
"I think" said Michael John, "that the best course of action is for us to drive to St Lucia police station. You two can drop me there to smooth things over with the authorities. You drive back to the river and return the beach buggy. If you meet an irate owner, then comfort him or her with money! I know it's a long walk for you but if you can't get a lift you'll just have to make it back on foot to the Paradise hotel which is slap in the middle of town; you can't miss it. Tomorrow we will make a plan to get to Durban."
With this he started the beach buggy and drove towards town at less than half the speed they have been doing in the opposite direction

It was past midnight when three weary figures entered the reception area of the hotel. The reception clerk half raised an eyebrow when noting that their only luggage was two briefcases and handed over two adjacent room keys.

All three slept the sleep of the dead and barely made it to the dining room for breakfast before it closed. From the hotel, they made their way to a nearby outfitters and bought a change of clothing. The problem of transport to Durban was easily solved as one of the major car hire companies had an agency in the town from which they leased a modest saloon on the agreement that they could turn it in at the firm's Durban office.

*****

The sun was hot and the air humid as the car ate up the kilometres down through Zululand. Connie questioned Michael John, "How did you convince the police so easily?"
"No problem really," replied Michael John, "the sergeant on duty was half asleep and barely questioned my story. I told him that you two were tourists in Zimbabwe whom I met and who had agreed to help me get out of Mozambique with my boat. Our presence in St Lucia, I explained as due to engine trouble as we were heading to Durban. I didn't complicate matters by mentioning Courtney and the explosion on the boat I convinced the sergeant was probably caused by a gas leak in the refrigerator or deep-freeze. The sergeant obviously didn't want his life made more difficult and so apart from making a note of our passport numbers and giving us forty eight hours to report to immigration and customs in Durban, was quite happy to see the back of me."
"It's simplified matters not having to explain why we nicked the beach buggy. The owner must have been aboard one of the boats moored in the river never noticed it's absence." added Connie.
"I still can't get over the way Courtney died, disgusting as he was, I felt sorry for him in those last few seconds on the bridge." mused Bonnie.
"Don't waste time and emotion on him. He got what he deserved and you two have now got what you deserve, the money and the emeralds. We have to work out a way of getting them out of South Africa and into Britain for you." said Michael John.

The road was almost deserted and the occupants of the car were able to sit back and relax as they gazed at the fascinating scenery. For kilometre after kilometre, they drove through a land of undulating hills carpeted with verdant sugarcane occasionally interspersed with darker green blocks of cultivated pine trees. The giant irrigation setups and the mansions set on hilltops spoke of wealth derived from the sweetness of the luscious game.

The city of Durban surprised the two women. Their approach from the north revealed stretches of golden sand bordered by tall buildings. The hotel on the beachfront that they checked into was a five-star one and compared with the best in Europe. Turbaned Indian staff padded silently across deep pile carpets. Michael John thought it fitting that their first meal, dinner, in the city more than half populated by Indians, should be a curry at the Golden Poppadom. In spite of the chilly hotness of the meal and partly because of a cool dry South African wine, an inner feeling of satisfaction and peace settled on the trio who made their way to the suite on the 19th floor shortly after nine o'clock.

With windows wide open and curtains undrawn a cool breeze played on the naked bodies who indulged themselves in what Bonnie sleepily described later as they lay sated as a "a mighty fine session of bedroom calisthenics".

*****

The heat haze hung over the beachfront as Michael John made his way to the parked car and from there to the customs and immigration offices near the harbour. He had firmly insisted that the presence of the girls was not necessary and so they took themselves off by bus to visit the Indian market.

Over a light lunch Bonnie and Connie enthused over the exotic oriental sights and smells they had experienced that morning. They marveled at the presence of hundreds of thousands of cheeky brown mynah birds and could not agree with Michael John's comment that they were an unmitigated pest.

Reluctantly Connie raised the matter of their departure: "I could go on living here with you forever, Michael John, but we must get the money back to London, sort out Max Cohen and get the orphanage off the book." she declared.

"I do think we should book air passages back home as soon as possible now." Agreed Bonnie.
"I'm one step ahead of you. I have booked you on an SAA flight tomorrow morning and if you come up to the bedroom, I'll show you how you're going to get the boodle into Britain." he said lightly.

In the suite on the 19th floor, Michael John removed a large parcel from one of the cupboards, "I bought this this morning" he said as he tore off the brown paper wrapping with a flourish to reveal a very dead stuffed crocodile of about one and a half metres in length.

The two girls stepped back in sheer horror.
"I think you've got a sick sense of humour" declared Connie angrily.
"Calm down, this is not a joke," said Michael John and went on to explain. "forget about the connection with Courtney. This revolting example of the taxidermist's art can have its belly seam cut open. We can pack the money and emeralds inside and then stitch it up again."
The two girls calmed down and saw the feasibility of his plan. Michael John continued, "I tell you what, you two take yourselves to the beach shop downstairs, buy yourselves a couple of itsy-bitsy bikinis and go soak up the sunshine on the beach. I'll open up this reptilian monster and pack him with the goodies." As he said this he looked at the stuffed crocodile which seemed to stare back at him malevolently through evil looking yellow glass eyes with black vertical slits of pupils.
"Okay! On one condition, you don't pack any of the two hundred thousand rand in South African currency into our friend here." said Connie cheerfully.

The dinner table was a scene of false gaiety. The wine they drank seemed sour compared to the night before. The crayfish thermidor did little to tickle their palates. With a feeling of slight embarrassment untempered by the wine he had drunk, Michael John raised a glass and toasted his two lovely companions.
"To the two most wonderful, resourceful and seductive angels I've ever

met. If I could make up my mind which one of you I love the most, I would propose here and now!"
Connie replied with, "to the mostest man I think that either of us has met, the greatest fighter and the greatest lover, Captain Michael John Dunne!"
Bonnie raised her glass and added, "to St Mark's, Jannie and Lucky. Which reminds me, don't you think we should phone Jannie and tell him everything is fine !"
Connie answered her. "I think it's time to tell Michael John that we're handing over the two hundred thousand rand to him. Michael John, we want you to send Jannie fifty thousand rand to buy himself a garage and the balance is for you."
Michael John looked sheepish as he mumbled, "I don't need all that money, I'm going to get myself a job here in Durban. By all means give Jannie the fifty thousand but remember that you two don't owe me a cent. You gave me something money can't buy, a new lease on life."
"Nonsense!" Said Connie firmly, "we decided and that's that!"
Bonnie hastened to add, "if we weren't committed to Max and the orphanage we would give you more !"

That night, their last night together, they made love only for a short time but with an ardency that anticipated the pain each would feel on parting the following day.

The departure of the girls at the reworked airport was a time of great sadness. The raw passion and love that was evidenced as Michael John embraced first Bonnie and then Connie, shocked some of the elderly passengers but the participants were oblivious.

Chapter 21

Through the aeroplane's window Connie who had the window seat, could see nothing but grey cloud. As the sound of the engines reversing thrust rose to a high pitch, the 747 dropped below cloud level into a steady drizzle which considerably reduced visibility. The landing lights momentarily seen on the final approach, shone bravely through the gloom. As the wheels touched the runway, one could imagine but neither see nor hear the spray of water being flung aside by the fast moving wheels.

The aircraft door opened to allow entry to an icy blast of damp air. Connie and Bonnie reached for their coats and donned them gratefully before proceeding to the exit. The scene before them was utterly depressing. It was as if a painter had applied a grey wash to the picture which was before them. The contrast with the Gaugin-like vivid colours and marked division between light and shadow of the continent they had left behind was almost too much for their minds to adjust to.

The crocodile caused more mirth than official concern when, having been retrieved along with their luggage, it was presented to the customs official. Again, it passed the security scan in innocence, it's easy passage perhaps made easier by the subtle flash of leg below a very short woolen miniskirt which was" accidentally" revealed as Bonnie "just happened" to catch the edge of her coat on the corner of the customs officials desk. He waved them through with the cheery comment, "I see you brought your supper back with you!" He turned away with no more thought for the crocodile.

The taxi driver outside the terminal was more vociferous about the crocodile.
"That's not coming in my bloody cab! This is a taxi not a bloody circus van!" he said.
Connie sweetened his disposition with two fivers and as she and Bonnie

climbed into the cab, ordered, "to Queens Gardens and quick, Buster, or I'll set the croc on you!"

To Bonnie and Connie, the flat and its familiar surroundings appeared to have a serenity and normality to it that seemed alien in the face of the events of the last few weeks. Nevertheless, they were happy to return. The success of their mission and the excitement over what had taken place in southern Africa induced in them a lethargy and feeling of laissez-faire and consequently they did not hurry to contact Max Cohen and Father O'Meara in their first evening home.

*****

It was the following morning that they decided to open the crocodile and retrieve the money for delivery to Max. Bonnie took a pair of scissors and cut a section of the stitches. She eagerly tore away the foil lining and wood wool, her hands exploring the inside of the crocodile. Finding nothing, she ripped open more stitches and started to snatch out all the wood wool until nothing remained inside, literally nothing; the money and the emeralds were gone.

"I don't believe it. There must be some mistake!" cried Bonnie as she picked up a glass ashtray and hurled it at the mantelpiece.

"Michael John couldn't, wouldn't, but must have!" moaned Connie as she restrained herself from smashing another ashtray.

"The sodding bastard loved us, looted us and left us!" came from a now tearful Bonnie.

"Any belief I ever had in any member of the human race has now been destroyed. I just can't believe that such an apparently lovely person as Michael John could play such a dirty trick on us," lamented an equally tearful Connie.

Further lurid, vociferous descriptions of Michael John and his dubious

parentage were interrupted by the chimes of the front door bell. Connie went to answer it. There was no one there, but on the floor lay an envelope. She stooped to pick it up and tore it open as she returned to the living room.
"The world gone mad! "she declared, "we go halfway round the world, nearly get ourselves killed, failed to get the money so urgently needed by St Mark's and here arrives an invitation to a Christmas party at the orphanage this afternoon. I just don't get it." she said to Bonnie who listened in amazement, before grabbing the sheet of paper that Connie held to check that her friend was not the one who had gone mad.

The words confirmed Connie sanity.
"We can't go. How can we celebrate at the orphanage when we can't deliver the money to get it off the hook?" Bonnie complained.
"I suppose we will have to go and suffer our shame and Father O'Meara's disappointment." said Bonnie

*****

The church hall was highly festooned with colored lights and streamers. Inside, about fifty assorted children applied themselves to mounds of food of high calorific value. Small smiling faces sported masks of cream and jelly and chocolate. An unusually jovial Mother Kathleen greeted Connie and Bonnie at the door. In answer to Bonnie's query, she explained that father O'Meara would be late as he had been summoned to see the Bishop.

As the two girls walked into the hall with unsmiling faces that contrasted with the rest of the revelers, they were aware that one, the thinner, taller one of two Father Christmases was advancing on them.

Without a word he stepped up to Bonnie planted a rather whiskery kiss

straight on her lips. Bonnie pushed him away violently. Undaunted he turned to repeat the exercise with Connie. This time he failed completely as Connie swung her arm in a wide arc and caught him open palmed across the cheek. Father Christmas stumbled back and as he did so, his substantial white moustache and beard fell off. Michael John stood grinning at Bonnie and Connie. He was immediately aware of the unbridled hatred that showed in their faces and quickly backed away and said, "before you both blow a valve or annihilate me, take a look at these!"
With this he reached into the folds of his red robe and extracted two pieces of paper. He handed them to the two women. They each took one, opened it and read in amazement. The smaller piece of paper was a receipt signed by Max Cohen for the sum of £1,800,000. The second, more substantial document was the cancelled mortgage on St Mark's.
"I'm not finished" said Michael John quietly. He handed Bonnie a third piece of paper. She read it through a blur of tears: it was a cheque for £200,000.00.

Simultaneously Bonnie and Connie launched themselves at Michael John, embracing him with such wild abandon, that a 13-year-old spectator in her first bloom of acne turned to her companion with the wink and declared knowingly, "I bet I know what they're going to give him for Christmas!"

Bonnie and Connie led Michael John to a quiet corner of the hall.
"Why, Michael John, why the deception?" asked Bonnie trying to stem tears that trickled down her cheeks.
"It's a long and complicated story which will become clearer if I introduce you to somebody." With this he steered them over to the other Father Christmas who stood alone nearby.
"Girls, I want you to meet said Sir John Gallagher."
Sir John, who's white whiskers were real, bowed gracefully as he took each of their hands and turned and said in a firm and dignified voice, "Delighted to meet you my dears. Heard so much about you from

Michael John."

Once introductions were over, Michael John continued.
"The time has come to tell you the truth. Soon after I left the Selous Scouts, I was recruited by Sir John to work for his department, which is a hush-hush group who do a lot of dirty work for other government departments such as the Foreign Office and even Scotland Yard. As an agent in Zimbabwe, I was asked to find out who was supplying the large quantity of synthetic emeralds which were being passed as the genuine article all over England. I had actually not got anywhere until you two came along. The rest of the story you know."
"How did you get to London so quickly?" Demanded Bonnie.
"Simple" grinned Michael John, "I left on an Air France flight two hours after you. I must admit I've had to work pretty hard since I arrived, to see Max, persuade the Bishop to delay Father O'Meara and to organise the party."
"You mean to say that you were not a drunken bum and we wasted out time in the Vumba?" ground out Connie.
"Not exactly. I had genuinely gone a bit off the rails and was actually in danger of being fired by St John." came Michael John's reply.
"But why didn't you tell us who you worked and for why snaffle the money and the emeralds?" demanded Connie.
"Well first of all, Sir John's organization is a well-kept secret, secondly you hadn't a snowballs hope in hell of smuggling the money and emeralds into Britain, so I just sent them through in the diplomatic bag, no questions asked. Finally, I couldn't tell you that I was coming to London, on permanent recall as it happened, until I'd seen Sir John and discussed a proposition I think he had better make to you himself." explained Michael John.

Sir John now spoke: "Michael John thinks very highly of you two and on his recommendation, I would like to offer you both positions in our organization. You will receive a good salary, no public recognition for the often unpleasant jobs you do but I can promise you work that cannot

be equaled for diversity, excitement and even danger."
Bonnie and Connie looked at each other and smiles creased their faces.
"Done, Sir John!" said Connie.
Bonnie added with a wicked smile, "on one condition, Sir John: as long as you have no objection to three of your operatives cutting down on their living expenses by sharing a flat in Queens Gardens!"

A grey-haired figure was divesting himself of his overcoat at the entrance to the hall. Bonnie and Connie saw him at the same time and together rushed over to him. After each had planted a firm kiss on both his cheeks, they handed him the cancelled mortgage. Father O'Meara read it carefully and then looked up.
"You blessed darlings. I don't know what to say..."
He faltered and then continued in a broken voice, "me darling, darling angels, some may say tarnished angels, but I know as sure as I stand here, that he will have a place for you one day in the heavenly host".

Bonnie and Connie turned to face Michael John and it was Connie who said in a gentle voice: "I think too much credit is being heaped on us two unlikely angels and not enough on this bit of a devil here." With this the girls arranged themselves one on each side of Michael John and with arms wound tightly round his waist, steered him out of the hall.

Printed in Great Britain
by Amazon

78399093R00098